SET THE GALAXY ON FIRE

ON FIRE

TALES OF THE ORION WAR – VOLUME 1

M. D. Cooper

Because the story isn't finished yet...

An anthology of short stories set during and following the events of Destiny Lost.

If you haven't read Destiny Lost, I highly recommend that you do. These stories tie directly into the events at the end of Destiny Lost, and add color and depth to the next book, New Canaan.

I hope you enjoy these tales of the *Intrepid,* and beyond into the broader galaxy around them, where the news of the Battle of Bollam's World spreads like wildfire....

TABLE OF CONTENTS

THE WORLD OF AEON 14

For the seasoned science fiction reader, there will be little here which they have not seen in another story, be it planetary rings, nano technology, AI, or mind-to-mind communication.

However, for those who may not know what a HUD is, understand the properties of deuterium, or cannot name the stars within the Sirius system, I encourage you to check out the glossary at www.aeon14.com.

To get the latest news and access to free novellas and short stories, sign up on the Aeon 14 mailing list: http://www.aeon14.com/signup.

BOLLAM'S WAR

THE MORNING AFTER

STELLAR DATE: 10.29.8927 (Adjusted Years)
LOCATION: ISS *Intrepid*, **Orbiting Fierra**
REGION: Bollam's World System, Bollam's World Federation

Joe eased into his chair at the kitchen table and took a long pull of his coffee. Movement outside the window caught his attention, and he saw a group of squirrels fighting over nuts fallen from the oak in the backyard; their antics coaxed a laugh from him.

Above, inside the house, he heard the floors creak as Tanis readied herself for the day ahead. He wished upon her all the time in the world, though he knew that was not to be. This would be the day; they would make their move and leave Bollam's World for Ascella—and a meeting with the FGT.

The squeaks and groans moved across the ceiling above him and Tanis emerged on the stairs at the far side of the living room. She looked as young and sharp as the first day he had seen her in the section chief's office on the Mars Outer Shipyards.

Something that had impressed him at the time, given she had just been in a firefight.

She quickly skipped down the steps, her shipsuit crisp, boots polished, and hair pulled back in a ponytail that bounced along behind her. He always found the hairstyle incongruous with how she presented herself, but loved all her little idiosyncrasies and kept his thoughts to himself.

"Good morning, again," he said with a smile, and gestured to the cup of coffee on the table across from him.

Tanis returned the smile and collapsed into her chair, which groaned in protest.

"The chairs may be getting a bit old for such abuse," he said and shifted in his for emphasis. The wooden seat creaked in protest and Tanis inclined her head and shrugged.

"I'll add it to my list of things to do."

Joe pushed the plate containing pancakes and bacon toward her.

"You don't have to do anything. I'm sure we have a bevy of carpenters who would do anything to make a set of chairs for the General."

Tanis took a long drink from her cup and frowned. "I know, I know, but I like to do some things for myself—even more, now that I'm *The General*. It seems that I can't even get my own coffee anymore."

She winked at the last and Joe shrugged.

"I was up first. You would have done the same."

"I would have made the pot. I don't know that I would have poured you a cup. I didn't know when you'd be down, and I wouldn't have wanted it to get cold."

Joe inclined his head and nodded. It was a conversation they had had a thousand times. Sometimes when angry and irrational, other times when laughing and joking, and times, like today, when they were both feeling melancholy.

"So...about not leaving each other ever again," Joe said, his eyebrow raised and a wry smile on his lips.

"I know, I know," Tanis sighed. "I don't want you to go, but we both know you have to; there's no one better than you at the helm of the *Andromeda*."

"It's because Corsia thinks I'm hot," Joe chuckled and Tanis raised an eyebrow.

"That silicate hussy..."

Joe felt a frown crease his brow. "What?"

Tanis laughed, a sound he was glad to hear. Her laugh had been in short supply over the few days since her return to the *Intrepid*.

"It's something that Angela said to Helen when she tried to scope me out with her nano," Tanis replied.

"Now that's a scene I would have liked to see," Joe said.

"You really wouldn't have. I was a mess."

"I've seen you messy before," Joe said, his expression distant. Then he blinked and refocused on her. "What do you think of Sera and Helen, other than the part where you're pissed off that she won't tell you all her deep, dark, secrets?"

Tanis opened her mouth to speak, a harsh look crossing her face, but then she stopped herself and schooled her expression. "Sorry. You were right before. I should respect her privacy—it's the part where she has a secret that could risk the entire ship that bugs me. When I came on board, the captain knew my history, there were no secrets there."

"Fair enough," Joe said with a nod. "But it is still his call, and he's opted to take her up on her offer."

"Yeah," Tanis said with a sigh. "I told him to take her up on it, as well. She's never done wrong by me; risked her life for mine. Logic dictates that she will continue to do so—unless she's truly nefarious."

"So, that aside, what do you think of Sera and her AI? It seems like a pretty powerful pairing for this low-tech time we've found ourselves in."

Tanis leaned back in her chair, taking another drink from her cup before speaking. "You're right about their abilities. If they had nanocloud tech, I would say their whole package is more advanced than Angela's and mine. Helen is...weird. She reminds me of how Angela and I work, but I know that is because of other circumstances—ones that I can't believe would be manifest in someone I just happened to find on the far side of space."

"When I asked Priscilla about them, she said there was something unusual about Helen, but wouldn't say what," Joe replied.

"Did she?" Tanis asked. "Well, if she knows, Bob knows, and if he's not alarmed, then I guess I'm OK with it."

Joe rose from the table and cleaned up their plates, leaving them on the counter for an automaton to wash later. Tanis stood and embraced him as he turned.

"Be careful out there," she whispered in his ear.

Joe wrapped Tanis in a deep embrace. "And you stay in the system. No gallivanting around the galaxy."

"I won't go gallivanting anywhere without you, I promise," Tanis replied.

They held one another for several minutes before Joe pulled back and gazed into his wife's eyes.

"You be careful, too. You have precious cargo—and I'm not just talking about the colonists in stasis."

Tanis reached a hand down to her abdomen. "I will. I plan to stay on the *Intrepid's* bridge—in theory, the safest place in the fleet."

"So long as we win," Joe said.

Tanis pulled back and looked him in the eyes. "Of course we'll win. Haven't you heard? I'm lucky."

TO WAR

STELLAR DATE: 10.29.8927 (Adjusted Years)
LOCATION: ISS *Intrepid*, Orbiting Fierra
REGION: Bollam's World System, Bollam's World Federation

Joe stood on the dock, staring up at the *Andromeda*, mentally preparing himself for the day ahead. He may live on the *Intrepid*, but over the years, the *Andromeda* had begun to feel like *his* ship.

<*You checking me out, Commandant?*> Corsia asked.

Joe laughed and walked toward the ship. "You know I'm a one-woman man, Corsia…well, two, if you count Angela."

Corsia's laugh echoed in his mind. <*And I'm a one-man ship.*>

<*Sure you are,*> Joe replied with a smile, taking a measure of comfort in the familiar banter with Corsia.

Joe took a long walk around the cruiser, giving it a visual once over. It was far from necessary; as the ship's XO, Corsia had everything well in hand—she always did—but it was a ritual left over from his days as a fighter pilot. The *Andromeda* was under his command. Its capabilities and crew were his

17

responsibility, and he took that responsibility seriously.

He watched the loaders trundle the last of the relativistic missiles aboard the ship, bringing the total loadout to over three hundred. Tanis wasn't taking any chances—the *Andromeda* now held more missiles than the entire ISF fleet had possessed during the battle with the Sirians. She was counting on the *Andromeda's* near-invisibility to help seed them throughout the battlefield. Joe accepted the duty given him. He would much rather deliver RMs than be on the receiving end of the missiles.

Satisfied with his review, he took the lift to the gantry that ran to the *Andromeda's* central crew hatch. The airlock was wide open, and he strode through onto the ship's main deck. Everyone he passed was focused on their assigned tasks and duties, moving with a calm efficiency. He knew each member of his crew by name and, as he nodded his greetings, Joe was certain they could be trusted to bring about victory this day.

The *Andromeda* had always done the Intrepid Space Force proud; the men, women, and AIs who made up its crew didn't plan to sully that legacy today—even if there were four hostile navies waiting for them.

Joe entered the bridge and nodded to Petrov, who sat at the helm reviewing his checklists with Jim, the ship's chief engineer, standing at his side.

"Good morning, Captain," Petrov said in greeting. "Anxious to get out there?"

Joe nodded. "Good morning, Petrov, Jim. Everything on the up and up?"

Jim cast Joe an appraising look. "We're just working on mass rebalancing all those missiles we're taking on. We gotta make sure that when we use them, we pull evenly from the racks. I know you. You're going to put this ship through its paces, and I don't want something coming loose."

Joe raised a hand and chuckled. "I'll do my best to keep us flying straight. Most of our work will be lurking and sneaking. How's our outer shell looking?"

"The trial run we did the other day was a success. When our active dampening is on and we're running dark, these guys couldn't see us if we were right on top of them. I've made a few more adjustments, after seeing what their active scan looks like—I bet we could park on their hulls if we wanted to."

<Let's not test that theory,> Corsia said. <Their hulls are where they mount their guns.>

"Whatever you say, Cor," Jim replied with a faint smile.

<I see how it is,> Joe said to Corsia with a laugh. *<I'm just a convenient alternative to Jim when he's busy.>*

<You know you've always been my side-human,> Corsia's mental avatar smiled. *<You know, two days ago, Jim and I celebrated a century since we first met— well, a century for him.>*

<I hadn't realized, congrats!> Joe replied.

<We didn't make a big deal of it, there are bigger things going on.>

<And you've been married for, what...seventy years?> Joe asked.

<Seventy four, and if you forget our seventy fifth when it rolls around next year, I'll be miffed.>

<Duly noted,> Joe said with a chuckle.

He remembered when he first met Corsia back in the Sol System. It was upon her arrival at the Cho, for delivery to the *Intrepid*. The memory amused him now—he had questioned Tanis on the need for a ship with offensive weapons. While the *Andromeda* had not—at least, not back then—been built entirely for combat, she was not like the other in-system transports that they were taking on.

Tanis had just laughed and told him that he was naïve if he thought that a colony in the millions wouldn't need a ship with some military capabilities.

After he learned of the picotech, the procurement of the *Andromeda* had made a lot more sense.

Jim, he met much later—not until after Tanis had defeated the Sirian cruiser in Kapteyn's System. At the time, he was just a civilian engineer, but Joe had forced him into the military academy in Kapteyn's System, and the man was now an ISF Master Chief.

Jim responded, bringing Joe back to the present.

"All looks well," the chief engineer said and glanced back at Joe. "Keep us safe out there."

"Always," Joe replied before the holoprojection of Jim winked out.

<You'd better,> Jim said over the Link from his station down in engineering.

Joe ran through his own checklists while the rest of the bridge crew filtered in, each of them early and looking a bit anxious.

The first to arrive were Trevor and Tori; two men, who, while not brothers by birth, had become as inseparable as twins. Trevor managed scan, and Tori worked weapons and tactics. They knew the

Andromeda as well as Corsia. Their AIs, Gwen and Aaron, were excellent complements, who managed comm and backed Corsia up with general ship management when under fire.

Last to arrive, though still ten minutes early for her shift, was Ylonda.

Ylonda appeared to be a slender woman in her twenties, but as an AI who chose to wear a human-like body, she was anything but what she appeared. Her AI mind was born of many parents—the norm for their species—but most notably, from Corsia and Jim.

Normally Joe wouldn't allow children to serve with their parents, but Ylonda had proven herself to be nothing but professional, and her behavior, thus far, had been above reproach; he also felt like what was 'normal' was less and less relevant every day.

He greeted each member of the bridge crew as they entered and set about their work. In the efficient manner he had come to expect, their tasks and duties required for departure were done well ahead of the allotted times.

<Looks like we're ready to go early, once again,> Corsia observed.

"Of course we are," Joe replied. "Ylonda, inform docking control that we're ready to hit the bricks."

Ylonda cast him the briefest of curious looks before replying. "Hit the bricks, yes sir."

Joe gave a soft chuckle and Corsia chided him. *<At some point, you're going to run out of new ways to say, "take us out," and that will be a good day.>*

<Never going to happen,> Joe replied. *<I could do them all day and never repeat a single one.>*

<Can I request a transfer then?> Corsia asked.

<Nope.>

"Permission to undock received," Ylonda supplied verbally while sending the departure parameters to Petrov's console.

"Here we go," Joe said with a smile, as the ship gently lifted from its cradle and drifted down the lane toward the ES shield at the end of the bay.

The *Andromeda* slipped silently into the darkness, and, with the smallest amount of thrust possible, moved toward its position between the *Intrepid* and the pirate fleet, which lay beyond Fierra's south pole.

They hadn't been underway for even a minute before Trevor spoke up.

"Looks like one of the new Arc-6s is having a problem," he said and threw his console's scan data on the bridge's main holo tank.

Joe looked up the squadron and saw that it was the Black Death; part of the wing normally stationed aboard the *Andromeda,* though operating under Fleetcom's direct control for this engagement. Concern filled his mind—he knew each of those pilots personally.

"Who is it," he asked.

"Cary," Ylonda supplied. "Fleetcom is directing us to move in under stealth and be prepared to assist."

Joe didn't know if he was happy that it wasn't Jessica, or worried that his friend would now put herself at risk trying to save one of her fellow pilots.

"Do it," Joe directed, and felt the ship shift under him as it moved toward Fierra's south pole.

Trevor updated the holo with scan data pulled from the fighter squadron, and he discerned the squadron commander's plan. Rock was going to have his ships shield Cary's fighter and push straight through the pirate fleet. It was a risky play, but given Cary's trajectory, there were few other options.

Joe felt a pang of regret as he watched the *Excelsior Nova* boost hard into position beyond the pirate ships, ready to catch the disabled Arc-6 fighter. That should have been Troy in the *Excelsior* down there; while he liked Nuwen, the ship's AI pilot, he had always held a warm place in his heart for Troy, and all the time he and Tanis had spent on the heavy lifter.

"Those pirates aren't going to just sit there," Joe said. "Let's do a flyby and drop off a few of our presents for them."

"How many are you thinking?" Tori asked.

"My analysis shows that eighteen is enough to disable most of their shields. Why don't you add four more for good measure?"

"Aye, Captain," Tori replied and bent to his task.

Joe knew that the estimation of how many missiles were required was, at best, an educated guess based on the data Sabrina and Helen had provided. However, he did know that the 89th century was unprepared for the type of warhead that the *Andromeda* carried.

Normal relativistic missiles achieved near-luminal speeds, and delivered their energy purely through kinetic force. The rail-delivered round released a massive amount of energy on impact— usually an order of magnitude more than a fusion bomb's energy. These missiles packed an extra punch. After the initial kinetic strike, the energy would trigger a secondary effect, causing the vessel of liquid metallic hydrogen within the missile to undergo fusion. The goal was to disable shields with the kinetic strike, and obliterate the enemy ship with the subsequent nuclear explosion.

Getting the materials for the secondary explosion to survive the kinetic impact had been a closely guarded secret of the Terran Space Force in Sol, but Earnest had figured it out back in Victoria; now the *Andromeda* carried hundreds of the advanced weapons.

"Captain, some of the enemy corvettes are advancing," Trevor announced.

<*Five, to be exact,*> Gwen, his AI, added.

"What are they doing?" Joe mused as he leaned forward in his chair. "They're moving slowly…like they expect to capture her."

"Eight fighters moving in to intercept them," Trevor reported aloud as everyone watched the action unfold on the holo tank.

"Wow, they are boosting *hard*," Petrov said with a whistle. "I guess those inertial dampeners are the real deal."

Joe nodded in silent agreement, mentally praying that the shields would work as well, because the tags on the holo display told him that Jessica was in the formation.

The engagement was energetic, and over in seconds.

The Arc-6s flipped their engines and boosted hard to re-engage the pirate corvettes. The fighters appeared to be intact, and none of the corvettes had taken significant damage, either.

Then, the fighters did something he would never have expected.

Almost lazily, they drifted over the enemy ships and dropped directly into their engine wash—a maneuver that would normally be fatal. There was a brief moment where the Arc-6s paused, and then the five enemy ships exploded.

"Ho-lee shiiit!" Trevor cried out. "Did you see that? They just…what the hell did they even do?"

"Something that's not in any book," Joe said and shook his head. A fighter that was impervious to kinetics, beam-fire, and gamma rays coming out of an AP engine? It was a game-changer.

"If those pirates know what's good for them, they'll bugger off now," Trevor grinned, and Joe shot him a stern look. "Uh… Captain," he added.

"No such luck," Ylonda said. "They're moving to engage. It doesn't make sense, why would they do that?"

"Because their armada has over two hundred corvettes and cruisers against forty fighters," Joe replied. "There's no scenario that existed, before five minutes ago, where they would be in any danger."

"But it's not five minutes ago, Captain," Ylonda replied.

"Some people are slow to catch up to reality," Tori supplied. "Besides, if we didn't have Fleetcom data telling us those fighters are in tip-top shape, none of us would believe they could do that again."

The bridge fell silent as every ship in the pirate fleet opened fire on the Black Death squadron, which had formed up in a protective cocoon around Cary's ship. The barrage obscured the Arc-6 fighters, and when the seven-second salvo ended, scan refreshed and the squadron came into view, intact and undamaged.

Cheers erupted on the bridge and Joe breathed a sigh of relief.

"Fleetcom has provided updated data. Their reactors are running too hot to survive another attack of that magnitude," Ylonda said.

"So, there *is* a limit to what these shields can take," Joe mused, as they watched the pirate fleet break into two groups and loop around to engage the fighters from both sides.

The crew looked to him, and Joe shook his head. The orders from Fleetcom were to stay clear while the *Enterprise* and *Defiance* filled the paths of the enemy ships with kinetic grapeshot. He passed control of the relativistic missiles they had seeded to Fleetcom, and sat back to watch.

The timing had to be perfectly coordinated, but if it worked, this rag-tag flotilla of pirate ships wouldn't be bothering them again.

It was as though the scene unfolded in slow motion on the holo tank. The lead ships of the enemy fleet hit the grapeshot and their shields held for a moment before the kinetic pellets began to slip through. A second later, their shields failed entirely, and the lead ships were torn to ribbons. Even one of the larger cruisers disintegrated under the assault, and Joe found himself hoping that whoever had tortured Tanis during her captivity was on board.

Then the twenty-two relativistic missiles came to life; powerful engines boosting them toward the pirate fleet, and striking the ships that had taken the least damage from the grapeshot.

Explosions from the kinetic strikes and nuclear fire obscured the entire pirate fleet. When the radioactive haze cleared enough for scan to get a clear look, less than fifty ships remained operational.

Another round of cheers sounded on the *Andromeda's* bridge, and Joe joined in with his crew.

"Now *that's* how you take out a fleet!" Tori hollered.

"OK, people, settle down, we still have work to do out here. That was the weakest, most poorly organized enemy on the field. You can bet that everyone else just learned a lot about our tactics and is adjusting theirs." Joe cautioned his bridge crew.

They nodded and bent to their tasks while he opened a connection to the *Intrepid*.

<Nice work on the timing there, dear,> he said. *<Everyone sure is happy to have you back.>*

<That was mostly Angela; I'm just along for the ride,> Tanis replied.

<Don't listen to her for a second,> Angela broke in. *<It was her call to wipe them out like that, and after what they did to us, I don't feel any remorse.>*

<They overreached and got what they deserved,> Joe replied. *<What's next on the menu?>*

<Drop a few more of your presents off near Rebecca's fleet, then take up station on the far side of the Intrepid. *I expect the Bollers to make a move soon.>*

<*You got it,*> Joe said and closed the connection with a mental embrace. <*Do us proud.*>

THE ADMIRAL'S RETURN

STELLAR DATE: 10.29.8927 (Adjusted Years)
LOCATION: BWSS *Freya*, Near Kithari's L4
REGION: Bollam's World System, Bollam's World Federation

Captain Ren watched Admiral Senya storm onto the *Freya's* bridge, the rage on her face enough to keep even the boldest member of the crew from glancing at her.

"What the *fuck* just happened?" she hollered at Ren. "I thought things were under control out here!"

Ren ran a hand through his hair and held back a sigh. "They were. Our negotiations were going well; but then they got new intel, and everything changed. They have…some sort of shielding that we've never seen before. That pirate fleet couldn't even touch their fighters. The colonists wiped out over a hundred ships in five minutes."

"I can't believe the president didn't call me back sooner. What was he thinking, leaving me out in the Sidian Reach when the biggest prize we've ever seen drifts into our system?" She turned the full force of her gaze on Ren and he did his best not to flinch.

33

"I found out from a trader—a trader!—that our system was on lockdown and under siege from pirates—and the Hegemony, of all things."

Ren shifted uncomfortably and tried to look as if he agreed with the admiral. "That's unbelievable. I was under the impression they had sent for you immediately."

"Well, they didn't," Senya replied. "And then they put that fool Nespha in charge of the fleet. Of all the bone-headed things to do; he couldn't find his asshole to shit out of."

"Have the chiefs put you back in charge?" Ren asked, unsure whether or not he'd prefer it. If Senya was back in charge, there was no telling what she'd do; but if she wasn't, he'd have to listen to her rail for days.

"Of course they did," Senya cast him a cold look. <I have enough dirt on them to bury each and every one of those bastards. When this is over, I may do it anyway, just to punish them for trying to keep me away.>

Ren nodded solemnly, the only response he could think of. Admiral Senya was like a ticking time bomb; it was impossible to tell what would set her off. He never could tell if she behaved irrationally to keep those around her off-balance, or if she really was as unhinged as she acted.

Nevertheless, she commanded his division of the Bollam's World Space Force, and his cruiser was her flagship. It was a destiny conceived in hell.

There was little he could do about it; Senya had spent decades running her family's business interests and consolidating power, before setting her eyes on the military. With her deep pockets and intimate knowledge of the government's inner workings, she had risen through the ranks quickly, and was now the top admiral in the fleet.

It was only a matter of time before she moved on to seize the presidency.

The prospect did not excite Ren one iota, but there was no way he could stop Senya from getting anything she wanted. His only play was to make sure he didn't get steamrolled by her.

"We have an ambassador on board the *Intrepid*," Ren said. "We could open a channel with their captain and resume negotiations."

"That's not the message I want to send," Senya said with a smirk. "Recall our ambassador and get me targeting options on the ships they've deployed. I want every rail in the system to pound them to dust."

"Sir?" Ren asked. "Is that wise? What if the legends are true?"

"If the legends were true, the Victorians would have been able to defend themselves. Our people came from Sirius, and that ship was their enemy. They stole from our people then; they'll not steal from us now."

* * * * *

<You have to do something to stop her,> Nespha said to Ren over a private connection.

<There's nothing I **can** do; you know how she gets. Admiral Senya is determined to seize the Intrepid by force.>

Nespha's avatar sighed in Ren's mind. <And what of The Mark? Is she planning to let them ruin her prize?>

<Senya believes that the kinetic rounds will destroy some of the colonist ships, at the least. Then The Mark will move in. When they're fully engaged, we'll come in and get rid of those pirates and claim the colony ship.>

Ren waited for Nespha to respond. He didn't like having this conversation with the other admiral—Senya would have his hide if she knew—but refusing to respond to Nespha was not an option, either.

<I suppose that could work, unless those shields of theirs can withstand a kinetic strike. No one I have talked to has even heard of anything like them.>

<We'll know soon enough,> Ren replied. *<It's not their shields I'm worried about; it's what those AST dreadnaughts intend that concerns me. They didn't come here just to watch us duke it out.>*

<Agreed,> Nespha's tone was more dour than usual. *<They haven't responded to a single attempt at communication. Our tacticians think they're waiting for backup.>*

<I agree with that assessment, as does Senya. It's why she wants to take the Intrepid *as quickly as possible. Our window is closing quickly.>*

<We shall see,> Nespha replied before closing the connection.

Ren didn't know what to think of the conversation. Nespha didn't like Senya, but he had always treated fairly with Ren and the other captains. He wasn't a firebrand like Senya; he was cautious. Often too cautious. Senya may be nearly impossible to deal with, but she did get results.

PREPARATIONS

STELLAR DATE: 10.29.8927 (Adjusted Years)
LOCATION: ISS *Andromeda,* Near Fierra
REGION: Bollam's World System, Bollam's World Federation

In the wake of the pirate fleet's destruction, Tanis addressed the fleet.

Joe watched the *Andromeda's* bridge crew smile at one another and sit up straighter as they listened to Tanis's speech. The news that the FGT would meet with them, and that a colony world was still waiting, had the desired effect on their spirits.

The moment Tanis signed off, orders came in to reposition between the *Intrepid* and the Boller fleet. He passed the order on to Petrov who turned to look at him.

"Really, Captain? What, with that weird thing those other pirates are doing?"

"Comes from Fleetcom," Joe replied. "*Sabrina* is on its way out there to help out, too. They have the new stasis shields, so they should be able to take whatever that rag-tag armada throws at them."

<Careful, Joe,> Corsia cautioned privately. <We don't know enough to be cocky.>

<I'm not cocky, I'm angry. Those people were going to torture Tanis; they **did** torture Sera.> Even as Joe spoke, he knew his words were disingenuous. Tanis had told him of what she did to Kris and Trent; she was no stranger to torture, either.

<Anger is not a winning argument,> Corsia replied.

<You're right. I'm just on edge. I just got her back, and now we're apart again; out here…fighting for our lives once more.>

<Yes. And we'll win once more.>

Joe laughed. <Now who's cocky?>

* * * * *

Time passed slowly as the *Andromeda* passed behind Fierra before drifting out into the van of the forces positioned between the *Intrepid* and the Boller fleet.

"Petrov, let's lay in two lines of missiles. The first fifty-thousand klicks from the *Intrepid*, and the second at the two-fifty kay mark."

"You got it, Captain," Petrov replied, as he plotted a course and ran it past Corsia and Ylonda.

"I have the next batch racked and ready to drop, Captain," Tori added from the weapons console. "I recommend that we seed a dozen defense turrets out here, as well—keep any anti-missile fire from taking them out, if it comes to that."

"Save them for the next picket," Joe replied. "I just got word from Fleetcom that some tugs are going to pull out some meaty turrets to keep our birds safe."

"Oh, really?" Tori asked. "Are they those new rhinos?"

Joe nodded. "I guess they got them done sooner than they thought with some of the new grav-tech. They were able to solve the recoil issues that had necessitated more fuel than we had handy."

"Oh, that'll be good," Tori rubbed his hands. "I almost hope the Bollers get that far."

Petrov and Ylonda both sent a frown his way, and the weapon's officer shrugged. "What I can I say? I like to see things go boom."

Ylonda straightened in her seat; a physical gesture Joe had noticed her use lately when shifting her focus. He wondered if it was deliberate or affected.

"Orders from Fleetcom. Tactical suspects inbound kinetics," she said. "They're instituting an updated jinking pattern."

"Steady on," Joe said. "They can't see us, and jinking will give us away—just don't be predictable, Petrov."

"Aye, captain," the pilot replied.

"Those kinetics are a ballsy move," Tori commented. "What's their play, captain?"

Joe wanted to tell Tori to focus on the task at hand, but the entire crew had turned to him, curious to hear his response. Well, everyone except Petrov, though he could tell that the pilot was also listening by the way he cocked his head. His marriage to Tanis often made everyone think that he had direct access to the inner workings of her mind, and by extension, the minds of their enemies.

However, he didn't need Tanis's insight for this one.

"They can probably tell the difference between our regular shielding, and the Arc-6's shields, so they know that not all our ships have stasis shields. What they don't know is whether or not we just have them turned off at the moment. They also know that if all our ships have stasis shields, we will simply crush everyone and win. So a surprise attack with kinetics to take out any of our vessels that don't have stasis shielding right now is their best play."

"What about The Mark's fleet?" Trevor asked. "If they take out our ships, then those pirates will take the *Intrepid*."

<*I suspect that they plan to deal with The Mark themselves. Now that we got rid of Padre's fleet, it's a much simpler task. Speaking of tasks...*> Corsia added.

His crew remembered themselves, and everyone returned to their work to finish seeding the first line of relativistic missiles. Petrov was carefully maneuvering the ship to the location of the second line when Fleetcom confirmed the Boller kinetic attack.

"Looks like they had shots lined up on every one of our cruisers—except us, of course," Ylonda said.

<*The* Intrepid's *scan and data group is rather happy with themselves,*> Corsia added.

"I think the whole fleet is rather happy with them," Joe chuckled. "What's Fleetcom's response?"

"They're returning fire."

Joe widened the view of the Boller system on the main holo tank, watching as Fleet Tactical lit up targets. The ISF didn't have the firepower to deliver the type of slugs that the platforms back in Kapteyn's were—had been—capable of delivering, which made long-range shots at enemy ships impossible. However, the selected targets were stationary rail platforms positioned on moons and asteroids. Bodies that had predictable paths.

The holo lit up with shots as the fleet let fly their kinetic rounds at the enemy emplacements. A minute later, two hundred and sixty slugs sailed through space.

The ISF's ship-mounted railguns were much easier to detect than the ground-based ones. For starters, they moved the ships when they fired, and the vessels used thrusters or main engines—depending on the size of the slug—to compensate.

Because physics weren't willing to budge on this point, the Bollers saw the shots coming.

"They're scrambling to intercept our slugs," Trevor said from the scan console. "Our guys masked their trajectory well, though. I think enough will slip through."

DETECTION

STELLAR DATE: 10.29.8927 (Adjusted Years)
LOCATION: BWSS *Freya*, Near Kithari's L4
REGION: Bollam's World System, Bollam's World Federation

"They've picked up our rounds," the officer at the scan console announced. "Their ships are all moving to new positions outside of the pocket."

"What?" Senya yelled from across the bridge. "How is that possible?"

Ren felt a moment's pity for the woman operating the ship's scan, but strode over, curious as to how the colonists had detected the kinetic rounds in the darkness of space.

The scan officer shook her head. "I don't know. If I didn't know where they were, I wouldn't be able to detect them at all. But they're all going to miss."

Senya swore and Ren wondered if perhaps Nespha was right. The admiral seemed more emotionally invested in this battle than he would have expected.

No one spoke in the following minutes as the first of the slugs approached, then passed through the space where one of the enemy's larger cruisers *should* have been.

"They're repositioning," the scan officer announced. "Incoming kinetic rounds—they're targeting our stationary emplacements!"

"How do they know about those?" Ren asked, bewildered at how the enemy could have detected so many of their rail platforms so quickly.

"Don't worry about that; direct the fleet to take those slugs out. We know where *these* rounds are going!"

Ren passed the orders through the fleet AI, and directed his ship to fire slugs at the kinetic rounds passing closest to the *Freya*. His tactical group impressed him as they destroyed a half-dozen slugs and altered the trajectory of another ten with beam fire.

However, it wasn't enough. Dozens of the colonists' weapons were still going to get through and hit BWSF rail emplacements.

It was a disaster.

"Get me their commander," Senya yelled, and the comm officer scrambled to open a line of communication with the leader of the colony ship.

When the call was accepted, a holoprojection of a tall woman shimmered into view. Ren was surprised. He had not seen the leader of the colonists before, but he thought it was a man named Andrews.

The woman wore a military uniform; a general, by the stars on her lapels. Her long, blonde hair was pulled back tightly in a simple clasp and her cold blue eyes bore into Senya's with disapproval.

If Senya was curious about whom she was addressing, she didn't show it.

"You've just sentenced thousands of Bollam's citizens to death," Senya's voice dripped with venom. "There will be no more treaties. We will reclaim our new world, take your ship, whole or in pieces, and crush your pathetic little fleet."

The woman turned to address someone not visible on the holoprojection. "At least when we were dealing with the Sirians, they had proper megalomaniacs. This pales in comparison."

Ren watched Senya's face turn red. He suspected that she might have never had anyone disregard her in such a way. He knew what was coming, and steeled himself for the storm.

"Our ancestors were from Sirius! They got caught in Kapteyn's Streamer hundreds of years before you. They earned these worlds," Senya yelled and Ren realized that she had viewed the colonists as mortal enemies all along—though, such a view defied logic.

He glanced around to see the bridge crew's posture change; though they didn't turn or look toward Senya, he knew they were listening, and wondering where her rage would fall.

"Sirians…that explains a lot," the colonist woman said, her voice calm and controlled. "You say that we killed hundreds, but thousands would have died on our ships, had your kinetic rounds connected."

"They would not have!" the Senya replied, her voice rising in pitch. "You have advanced shielding, what we fired was merely a shot across the bow."

Ren knew this was not entirely true. Senya suspected that they may not all have the advanced shields their fighters had used when dealing with the pirate ships. Fleet Tactical's assessment was that if they did have them, there was no evidence to show they were activated. If the kinetics had remained undetected, they would have obliterated the colonist fleet.

On the holoprojection, the general scowled, her eyes narrowing into accusing slits.

"Are you seriously going to attempt to paint us as the aggressors? Until your unmistakable act of war, we had only taken defensive actions. You are brigands; you attempt to seize whatever drifts past your system to better yourselves. You're nothing more than well-established interstellar bandits."

Ren was barely able to make out the last of the general's words over Senya's screaming.

"You sanctimonious, dusty old bitch! Our people built this system out of nothing! We worked for millennia to create what you see! You would come here and pick our best worlds for yourselves in trade for trinkets. No one will have your tech; not those pirates, not those core-world bastards, and certainly not you! I'll see you all burn in h—"

Senya's words choked off abruptly as the holoprojection shut off, the enemy general disappearing from view.

Ren sucked in a deep breath as the admiral spun to him. "We're attacking. Ready the division!"

"Attacking, Sir?" Ren asked carefully.

"Yes, attacking. That thing you're all trained to do. We're going to crush those bastards and take their ship."

Ren was glad to hear that her proclamation of utter destruction was just for show, and nodded to his tactical officer to send out the orders. "Just our division?"

Senya had looked away in thought, but her sharp gaze snapped back to him. "Yes, just our division. Don't you think a hundred of our ships can take out a dozen colonist tugs and transports?"

Ren refrained from saying that the colonists possessed over two-dozen ships, and while they may have once been simple tugs and transports, they were now far more than that—they were highly advanced warships with unknown capabilities.

Not to mention those fighters. His division possessed no fighters, and only a smattering of combat drones. Senya may think that their victory was a foregone conclusion—and maybe it was—but how many would die for her to gain whatever strange revenge she was trying to achieve?

SUBTERFUGE

STELLAR DATE: 10.29.8927 (Adjusted Years)
LOCATION: ISS *Andromeda*, Near Kithari's Trojan Asteroids
REGION: Bollam's World System, Bollam's World Federation

"Boller fleet is on the move," Trevor announced.

"Fleetcom is directing us to move out and join the *Condor* in the Greek asteroids," Ylonda said.

"Do it," Joe directed.

The Bollam's World System was still young and hot, with the remains of stellar and planetary formation strewn everywhere. Unlike the Sol System, where things had settled down over billions of years, planets here—like Kithari, the gas giant near which the battle would take place—had not forced all their Trojan and Greek asteroids to fully settle into the planet's leading and trailing Lagrange points.

Instead, those two asteroid camps formed long smears of rock and debris leading and trailing the world—much of it very close, and very active. Space didn't present many large natural barriers you could take cover behind, but these regions of rock, sand, and dust were as close as it got.

Joe approved of Tanis's tactics. The cruisers would move out above and below the asteroid fields, while the fighters moved in closer to engage the enemy ships. The cruisers would surreptitiously seed the asteroid camps with missiles. When, inevitably, the ISF ships had to pull back, they would deliver a devastating blow to the enemy vessels.

"There are over sixty ships in range of our group," Trevor sounded nervous as he gave out the count. "No fighters, though; their smallest are corvettes, similar to what the pirates have—though more uniform in appearance."

"Steady. The General knows what she's doing. We're going to get through this and be on our way before you know it," Joe said in the calmest voice he could manage.

Two cruisers and a fighter shield against sixty capital ships were not the sort of odds he had ever expected to play.

"Shit!" Trevor's voice grew more alarmed. "Those pirate ships back there just did something...uh...weird...."

"It's a shield bubble," Joe provided. "Tanis informed me that they were planning to do that. Captain Espensen and the *Enterprise* are taking care of it with help from *Sabrina*."

"They better hurry up," Tori frowned as he pulled up a display of The Mark fleet's position relative to the *Intrepid's*. "It won't take long for those pirates to get to the *Intrepid*."

No kidding, Joe thought to himself.

Aloud, he did his best to bring the crew's focus back. "They have their jobs, we have ours. I want a hundred missiles in the leading edge of this asteroid camp, ASAP."

The Arc-5 fighters were engaging the Boller fleet as it approached the asteroids. This was Joe's least favorite form of space combat. Unlike the final battle with the Sirian fleet in the Kapteyn's System—which was characterized by brief, high-velocity engagements—this would be a slow-moving slugfest.

The Boller ships were boosting at a moderate speed, which would allow them to ease around Fierra and engage the *Intrepid*. The ISF defensive lines were almost at rest, relative to the Boller ships—ready to apply thrust and engage them as the enemy moved toward the *Intrepid*.

Much of the combat would occur with the ships barely moving relative to one another; it was the most deadly type of battle—missiles would easily seek their targets, and beams could track and penetrate targets with ease.

Already, Joe could see the *Condor* in the Greek asteroid camp, and the *Pike* and *Gilese* positioned in the Trojans, accelerating to gain erratic maneuvering options. No one wanted to be a sitting duck.

"The *Sabrina* is...it's running away," Trevor called out from the scan station.

<They wouldn't do that,> Corsia said with conviction. *<Sera's the sort that doesn't know when to stop—in my opinion.>*

"Agreed," Joe added. "I don't know them well, but Tanis trusts their captain with her life—has already done so on a few occasions. From what she's told me, Captain Sera even has a personal grudge against the leader of that pirate band. She has something up her sleeve," Joe wondered what that would be.

The crew's focus snapped back to their end of the battlefield as several of the missiles they had seeded at the edge of the asteroid camp came to life and sought out targets in the Boller fleet. The enemy took out two of the missiles, but another pair reached their targets—the kinetic impacts destroying shields and leaving the ships vulnerable to the secondary fusion explosion.

Unlike Padre's pirate fleet, the Boller ships were spaced hundreds of kilometers apart. There was little to no chance that any of the missiles would deal secondary damage. Still, two ships for four missiles was a good trade. If that ratio kept up, they could seriously weaken the enemy fleet.

The distance between the Boller ships would also lessen the danger of concentrated fire from an enemy fleet—if there had been an enemy fleet. The only two capital ships they were facing were the *Andromeda* and the *Condor*, and they couldn't even see the *Andromeda*.

The Arc-5s, on the other hand, were doing what they were made for; flying at extreme v and striking at a target before flitting on to the next. The Boller fleet's spacing—intended to protect them from capital ship beams—kept them from responding to the fighters in any serious measure.

Joe smiled to himself, growing even more grateful to the dust and rock permeating this primordial system. In an older, clear system, such as Sol, firing a beam across ten-thousand kilometers was child's play; but here, the beams, be they electrons or even more mass-heavy particle streams, were diffused by the time they reached their targets.

"They're having trouble targeting our fighters, Captain." Ylonda suddenly spoke up. "I don't think their algorithms are designed to track ships that move like ours."

"How so?" Petrov asked.

"We don't jink enough," Ylonda replied. "With every ship they face utilizing inertial dampeners; they have a lot of logic set aside to tell what is a feint and what is a real move. I suspect that no matter what our fighters do, it always looks like a feint to their AI."

"Good point. You should share that with our tactical groups," Joe said.

"I already have, Captain," Ylonda said and her face slipped into a slight frown. "It would appear I was not the first entity to make that assessment."

Joe chuckled. "Faster than I would have spotted it. Top marks from me."

Ylonda let a rare smile slip and nodded her thanks.

"Sweet fuck!" Trevor swore as a massive energy discharge lit up the holoprojection.

"What the hell was that?" Joe asked, rising from his chair.

"The...the...pirates...they're gone!"

Joe replayed the scan feed and realized that Sera had indeed not run from the fight. She had brought *Sabrina* back around Kithari and slammed her ship right into the pirate's shield bubble.

"So is *Sabrina*…" Joe said quietly.

"No!" Trevor called out, unable to keep the excitement from his voice. "The *Intrepid* spotted them. They're intact and alive."

Joe slumped back in his chair. "Thank the stars," he muttered. Then he sat up, Sera's gutsy move invigorating him. "Tori, drop four of our defense turrets. Let's make these Bollers see some ghosts."

Tori grinned. "Yes, sir. A bundle of Wrecking Balls on the way."

Joe watched Petrov coordinate the best drop-off placements for the WBs, and silently approved of his tactics. Petrov shifted the *Andromeda* into a trajectory where its engine wash dissipated in the asteroid camp, and boosted hard; leaving a wake of tumbling rock and swirling dust in its wake. There was no way the enemy could miss them, but that was the plan.

Four Wrecking Balls now lay along the path the *Andromeda* had taken. When they cleared the bulk of the dust and gravel, shields running hot, Petrov spun the ship, braked hard, then boosted on a new trajectory before repeating the maneuver.

Joe had always considered himself one of the best pilots in the ISF, but as Petrov moved the seven-hundred-meter cruiser, dancing it as if it was a ten-meter fighter, he wondered if his skill had been bested. Three minutes later, the *Andromeda* was a thousand kilometers from the fourth Wrecking Ball, and lost in a haze of confusion.

He wondered what the Bollers were thinking.

Except for its initial departure from the *Intrepid*, the *Andromeda* would have been invisible to the enemy for the entire engagement. Now they would see the wake and shadow of what they knew to be a cruiser; one that had been very close to the bulk of their fleet.

The majority of the enemy fleet was approaching the asteroids, and two cruisers—accompanied by six destroyers and over a dozen corvettes—broke off from the main force, searching for other ISF ships that may be lying invisible in the dust and gravel.

They passed by the first wrecking ball, and then the second. Everyone on the *Andromeda's* bridge waited—eager to see what would happen once the Boller ships became fully invested. The minutes ticked by slowly, and then the leading cruiser passed within a dozen kilometers of the fourth WB.

An enemy ship progressing that far was the pre-programmed signal. The balls spun to life, each firing beams at half a dozen targets while accelerating toward the closest enemy vessel. The WBs were not intended to provide long-term protection; just to allow enough time for the missiles seeded through the area to come to life and seek out their own targets.

However, for those few moments, they delivered as much punch as a mid-sized cruiser, fooling the enemy into thinking there were multiple ships in their midst.

The Bollers lashed out, destroying two of the WBs in an instant, and the third a second later. The fourth, the one closest to its target, collided with the enemy ship, pushing it off course and into a small field of gravel that lit up its shields.

That was all the time the relativistic missiles needed to achieve speeds over a tenth the speed of light, and to reach their targets.

Not every missile made it. The Bollers were on guard, and struck down nearly half. But those that did punch through shields, dealt lethal damage. The two cruisers remained intact; though the one that took a hit from the Wrecking Ball saw its shields fail, leaving it vulnerable in the field of gravel it now rested in.

Joe gave Tori the signal over the link, and his weapons officer launched two more missiles from the *Andromeda's* store at the crippled ship.

Two minutes later, only one cruiser from the exploratory force remained, moving out of the asteroids and back to the main Boller force.

"There," Trevor pointed to the main tank. "Ylonda, what do you think?"

Joe looked to his scan and comm officers. "What is it?"

"We think that cruiser is their flag. It has nearly twice the comm traffic as the rest of the ships, and its position in their fleet shows that they are guarding it."

"Except that it's in the group assaulting the ISF," Joe replied. That doesn't seem like the smartest thing to have your flagship doing.

"Nothing they are doing seems like the smartest thing," Ylonda replied. "They could have treated fairly with us and had better technology than any system in the galaxy. But now they'll have nothing."

Joe held back a laugh. Ylonda was picking up a bit of her mother's attitude.

PURSUIT

STELLAR DATE: 10.30.8927 (Adjusted Years)
LOCATION: BWSS *Freya,* Near Kithari's Trojan Asteroids
REGION: Bollam's World System, Bollam's World Federation

"There!" the officer on scan called out. "I have its position!"

Ren strode to the woman's side and looked over her data. Sure enough, there was a faint ion trail glowing in the dust near the edge of the asteroid camp.

"It lines up with where we saw the last two missiles come from," Ren nodded.

"I want that ship dead," Senya's venomous voice spoke over his shoulder. "Move in, we're taking it out."

"Sir," Ren said. "We just watched it destroy nearly twenty of our ships; we need to move cautiously."

"Captain," Senya's voice turned to ice. "Move the *Freya* toward that colonist piece of garbage and take it out. Bring the rest of the battlegroup with us."

Ren passed the order to his comm officer and pilot. Normally a fleet admiral would have her own staff to manage fleet coordination, but Senya's staff had not made it to the *Freya* with her, and she used his as though it were no inconvenience at all.

Not the greatest tactician in the BWSF, Senya won most battles through the brute application of force; though most times, she managed to undercut her enemies politically before things ever came to blows.

That meant it was up to Ren to organize the fifty-ship battlegroup to seek out and destroy the enemy cruiser.

<What is she up to?> Nespha's querying voice entered his mind.

<We have picked up the location of their invisible cruiser,> Ren replied. *<She's going after it personally.>*

<One trap wasn't enough for her?> Nespha asked. *<She needs to see if there's another out there?>*

"Captain Ren," Senya said, pulling his thoughts from the conversation with Nespha. "I want the other four battlegroups in this division to push in, as well. We'll overwhelm them and end this."

"Yes, sir," Ren responded and sent the orders on to the other battlegroup commanders, assigning his division's AI to manage the tactics while he responded to Nespha, who was signaling him with more questions.

<What is she doing?> the other admiral asked. <We're losing too many ships; it's going to leave us exposed to those dreadnaughts.>

<We **are** winning,> Ren replied, growing annoyed with Nespha. If the man wanted to confront Senya, he should do it directly; not through him. <Few of their ships have those impenetrable shields, and the rest just fall back rather than fight.>

<But fall back to what?> Nespha asked. <We don't know what other weapons they have at their disposal.>

<This is war, Admiral; we don't know what's coming next. I'm not excited about rushing into this battle, either, but I don't have a choice. Now if you'll allow it, I have a ship to run.>

Nespha didn't respond, and Ren hoped he would leave him alone. He didn't disagree with Nespha, but disobeying a direct order from his commanding officer was treason; his people had a better chance of surviving with him as a buffer between them and Senya's orders.

He examined the region of space on the holo tank, and directed two elements of his battlegroup to arc above and below the asteroids. He would bring the bulk of their forces around the asteroids on the planetary plane and catch the enemy ship from three sides.

Provided there *was* just one of them.

There was an upper limit to how many ships the *Intrepid* could carry. While the fleet the colony ship had disgorged was surprising in size and strength, it was not impossible to believe that they could house many more vessels. For all he knew, the bulk of their fleet was comprised of these stealth ships, and there was a dozen of them lying in wait.

Just as disconcerting were the missiles they were using. His tactical group had determined that somehow, they were able to shield a fusion device during the missile's kinetic strike, and then detonate that device in the moments a ship's shields flickered.

No one wanted to be hit by a relativistic missile, but it was an event that their ships—at least the destroyers and cruisers—should be able to weather on full shields. However, these missiles and their one-two punch were more powerful than any he had ever witnessed before.

He reminded the captains in his battlegroup of this, and directed them to increase their distance from one another—the enemy fighter's tactics had caused the fleet to bunch up.

The bridge was silent as the ships moved past the asteroids and toward the empty space that lay between them and Kithari...and the *Intrepid*. The enemy fighters were falling back to provide close support for their cruisers, and he prayed there were no surprises left behind.

Ren directed his ships to deploy any combat and sensor drones they still had to sniff out whatever they could in the asteroid field. His ships found two dormant missiles and destroyed them, but amidst the hot gas and wreckage from the previous incursion, it was difficult to find anything else.

"Were those just leftovers, or is there another wave of those damn things in there?" Senya asked from his side.

Ren glanced over at the admiral. Perhaps she really was thinking of the tactics behind the situation.

"Hard to say. The fact that they launched the final two missiles from their ship would make you believe that there were no more in the asteroids—until we just found those two."

"Sir, perhaps they were duds?" the tactical officer asked.

Senya cast the man one of her hard glares. "Do you think that these people have dud missiles? They've obviously geared themselves up for conquest as much as colonization."

"We'll know soon enough," Ren replied. "Be ready to fire chaff and all countermeasures at the first hint of an ion trail."

"Yes, sir—" the weapon's officer began before raising his voice. "Firing countermeasures! Multiple ion trails detected."

"How many?" Ren asked as he pulled the data onto the main tank.

He didn't hear the officer's response as he watched the display light up with over a hundred missile signatures.

It was going to be devastating.

The ships deployed every ounce of chaff and countermeasures they had at their disposal while firing at every signature they could lock onto. Dozens of the enemy missiles fell to their defenses, but many dozens more made it through.

The scan, tactics, and weapons officers worked frantically with their AI counterparts to stop the assault. When scan cleared, Ren saw that the majority of the fleet had survived unscathed; though many ships had suffered shield failures and minor impacts.

"Is that their best?" Senya asked and Ren glanced her way to see a hungry fire in her eyes.

Their moment of relief was brief as ships across the battlegroup began to suffer kinetic impacts and tear apart.

"What the fuck is that?" Senya swore and Ren enhanced the scan resolution, attempting to discern what invisible force was shredding the ships.

"Captain, it's...it's pebbles!" the scan officer called out.

"Pebbles?" Senya asked, confusion breaking the power she always projected in her voice.

Ren had read about this tactic, though he had never heard it employed.

"It's rail-fired pellets. They used to call it grapeshot," he said, watching in despair as every ship whose shields had failed under the assault from the missiles was shredded by the small kinetic impacts.

"I see that cruiser again," the scan officer called out. "It's on the move back toward the colony ship."

"Take it out," Senya growled. "Get that ship now!"

Ren had no option but to comply, though he noticed that some ships, which had reported engine failures, were able to brake and turn from the fight.

He wasn't sure if they were cowards, or far smarter than he.

MANEUVER

STELLAR DATE: 10.29.8927 (Adjusted Years)
LOCATION: ISS *Andromeda*, Near Kithari's Trojan Asteroids
REGION: Bollam's World System, Bollam's World Federation

"They've spotted us again, Captain," Trevor called out.

<At least fifty ships still moving in on our position,> Gwen added.

"We've gotta get clear so that Tanis can use the scoop to hammer them—I don't fancy being nearby when that happens," Joe said.

"With their pincer, we don't have a lot of options," Tori said.

"We can go through them, Captain," Petrov said without turning. "Drive right up the middle, firing on their flagship."

"I don't know if you've forgotten," Ylonda said. "We don't have a stasis shield."

"We won't have any shields if we stay here," Petrov replied. "We can get a flight of Arc-5s to give us cover."

Joe nodded. "Tori, get Jim to prep the chaff on the rails. We have five minutes before we're at max burn."

Tori nodded, and the bridge crew set to their tasks: coordinating with the fleet, arranging the fighter cover, and loading the last of their RMs into the tubes.

<You sure about this?> Jim asked from engineering. *<We're one ship against fifty—in case you'd forgotten.>*

<Didn't you hear Tanis's speech?> Joe replied. *<Be bold.>*

Jim chuckled. *<I suppose, she's never steered us wrong.>*

*<I don't know if I meant for you to be **that** bold,>* Tanis said privately to Joe.

<It's good to hear your voice,> Joe replied. *<I mean…I hear your voice on the fleet net, but it's a different you.>*

He felt Tanis's agreement as her support filled his mind. *<You can pull back; there's an escape vector you can take.>*

<I know,> Joe replied. *<But this crazy admiral of theirs has to be stopped. If she rallies the rest of their fleet, we'll be doing this all over again, and we don't have the RMs for that.>*

<I better see you for dinner tonight,> Tanis replied and ended the direct communication with a mental embrace.

Joe brought his focus back to his bridge. Everything was ready a minute early, and he directed Petrov to begin his burn.

Under normal circumstances, this attack run would be suicide; but of the remaining fifty ships advancing on the *Intrepid,* only twenty were within range of the *Andromeda,* and most of those did not yet have their shields up to full strength.

With the assistance of twenty Arc-5s, the maneuver was downgraded to merely insane.

Petrov ramped up the *Andromeda's* burn, bringing the fusion and AP engines to their max output. Thirty *gs* of force pushed everyone back into their seats and Joe smiled to himself. This was what flying in the black was all about.

The enemy ships came into range, and beams lanced out, playing across the *Andromeda's* shields— some penetrating and burning away ablative plating.

Tori fired the reflective chaff from the ship's rail guns, flashing it ahead of the cruiser and wreaking havoc on the enemy targeting systems. To their scans, the *Andromeda* was now lost in a massive cloud. The Arc-5s flitted about within the expanding wave of chaff, firing their beams and missiles at the enemy ships, and masking their true location, which was no longer in the center of the cloud.

Joe wondered what it would be like to be on the Boller flagship, watching a huge cloud of reflective chaff racing toward you, unable to see the ship you know must be within.

Several of the enemy destroyers pulled ahead, moving into the cloud to seek out the *Andromeda*, and Corsia let fly the last four of the ship's relativistic missiles.

The weapons didn't have time to achieve significant speed, but their nuclear blasts were enough to disable two of the destroyers and push the others off course.

The explosions disrupted the chaff cloud, and out of it flew the *Andromeda*, located near the bottom of the cloud's cover. They were seconds away from the enemy's flagship, and Joe watched as Tori and Corsia prepared to fire while Ylonda coordinated with the fighters.

Every rail and beam on the ship and the Arc-5s fired at once, overwhelming the Boller cruiser's shields and tearing through its hull. For a moment, the ship held; but then, in a blaze of fire, plasma, and shrapnel, it flew apart when its reactor's housing was breached, and a nuclear plume filled the space where it had been.

The fighters let fly their beams and missiles at several other ships, and then the formation was past the Boller fleet. The *Intrepid* lashed out with its MDC, killing the shields on the remaining ships and disabling many.

The *Andromeda's* bridge erupted in cries of joy and amazement, as Petrov dialed back the thrust and the crew leapt from their seats to slap hands and embrace one another.

Joe stood and smiled at his bridge crew.

"Well done, people, well done. Petrov, take us home."

ROOM WITH A VIEW
STELLAR DATE: 11.06.8927 (Adjusted Years)
LOCATION: ISS *Intrepid*
REGION: Interstellar Dark Layer near Bollam's World

Several days after the **Intrepid***'s first FTL jump...*

Joe took a moment to take in the sight of his wife as they exited the maglev train and walked across the small station platform to the corridor beyond.

Tanis was only three months pregnant, and wasn't showing yet, but there was a glow about her; a new elegance to the way she moved. He wondered if his reaction was due to evolution—a million years of human instinct built up to revere and protect pregnant females. But Joe knew that wasn't it. She *was* moving differently, subconsciously protective of her precious cargo, and proud of her ability to create a new life.

The dress she wore was one he had bought for her years ago from a shop in Landfall. He picked it because it reminded him of the one she wore for the first VIP event on the *Intrepid*, when they were attacked by mercenaries. That gown didn't survive the night and she had worn her dress blues for all following events, insisting that it was all the fancy clothing she needed—and far more practical.

Tanis wore her uniforms a bit tighter than regulation suggested, so Joe never minded, but he did like how she looked when she did herself up. When he asked her to wear the dress to dinner tonight, she smiled and did as he asked, knowing him well enough to understand where his head was at.

He trailed behind for a moment, taking one last look at how the shimmering red fabric slid across her ass, before catching up and linking his arm with hers as they walked sedately down the corridor.

"Wow, they put it back together just the way it was!" Tanis exclaimed as they entered the bow lounge above the ramscoop emitter.

"Yeah," Joe replied. "I hear that the scoop techs weren't about to lose their little piece of heaven just because some little pebble blew it clear off the ship."

Tanis smiled at Joe and he got that warm feeling that started in his toes. Even after all these years, she could still cause his heart to feel like it skipped a beat. Maybe it was because he still felt as if there was an element of mystery to her. Like Tanis was a wild animal at heart, and there was no way to ever tame her.

That was fine by him.

Tanis slipped past several other guests in the lounge and he followed her to the bar, taking a seat beside her as the servitor handed them paper menus.

"Thanks, Steve," Joe nodded to the servitor.

Tanis laughed and shook her head. The servitor didn't actually have a name, but they had unofficially granted him one during those long years the ship drifted toward The Kap. By some miracle, he had survived the lounge's near total destruction when the ship exited the Kapteyn's Streamer. Seeing him there, pouring drinks as though nothing had changed, gave them both some measure of happiness.

"Paper...huh," Tanis said and Joe nodded, feeling the coarse cellulose fibers between his fingers.

"From the flooding in the cylinders after we hit that pebble. It gave the ship a pretty good shake, and the lakes and rivers jumped their banks," Joe said. "The botanists decided to make paper from all the downed trees."

"Right, I remember reading that—and I did notice that the forest on the far side of the lake by our cabin starts a lot further from the shore than when I last saw it," Tanis replied.

They perused the menus for a while before Joe narrowed his choice down to just a few options.

"What are you going to have?" he asked.

"A soup I think; I need something to warm me up," Tanis said with a smile. "Not that you won't be doing that later."

"Would you like a drink to go with that, General?" the servitor asked. "We have a fantastic oaked chardonnay from the vineyard in Lil Sue that our other patrons have thoroughly enjoyed."

Joe watched Tanis give it some thought— perhaps double checking that her nano could filter the alcohol out before it made it to her baby—before replying. "Sure, let's go with that."

"Are you ready to order as well, sir?" the servitor asked Joe.

Joe studied the menu for a final moment. "Yes, Steve, I'll have the Jerhattan Strip, and a glass of your dark amber lager."

"You know, Bollam's was my fourth stellar system," Joe said as they watched Steve pour their drinks. "I only expected to ever see two."

"Lightweight," Tanis chuckled. "I've seen nine now."

Joe smiled in return. "I guess we're both lightweights in this age. I imagine Sera has seen hundreds of systems."

"At least," Tanis replied.

Steve set down their glasses and Joe raised his in a toast.

"To finally getting to *our* colony world," he said.

"To our colony world, wherever it may be," Tanis replied and clinked her fluted glass to the top of his tankard.

"Bets on where it is?" Joe asked.

Tanis flicked her wrist, deploying nano to create a silencing field around them.

Tanis let out a long sigh. "Honestly? Not a clue. I guess that I could ask Sera, but I'm still processing everything she told us. Somewhere in the Transcend, I suppose."

"The Transcend," Joe said with a shake of his head. "First we go from learning that humanity expanded from under a hundred extra-Solar colonies to tens of thousands. And now this; a second human civilization acting like gods out on the fringes of known space."

"Do you think what they're doing is wrong?" Tanis asked, her expression one of genuine curiosity.

Joe shrugged. "Who knows? From what Sera says, they started off honestly enough, just trying to keep themselves safe as the interstellar wars broke out. But you know how it goes: today's solutions are tomorrow's problems. Now they have this entirely separate civilization that's bigger in scope, if not in actual population, than the rest of humanity."

"And they encircle the Inner Stars," Tanis added. "They used to have a much larger buffer, but now the fringe nations are right up against the Transcend. It's a secret that is going to get out—and probably soon, too."

"Don't say that," Joe sighed. "I have a vision of us finally settling down and raising our little girl."

"What are we going to name her?" Tanis asked.

"Catharine," Joe said, the name already on the tip of his tongue.

Tanis turned her head and gave him a curious look, one eyebrow raised. "Catharine? Isn't that the name of your younger sister?"

Joe nodded in response. "In fact, I have *two* sisters named Catharine —my mother really liked the name. They were both good kids..." he trailed off as the knowledge resurfaced that all his brothers and sisters, his mother's great brood, were all long dead.

Tanis took his hand in hers. "Sucks, doesn't it?"

Joe took a deep breath. "Sure does, I mean, it's stupid, really...we didn't expect to see them again...but we didn't expect them all to already be dead for millennia either."

"Yeah, that's crossed my mind more than once, as well," Tanis replied. "It's silly, but I had always hoped to see Katrina again."

Joe nodded slowly, remembering the bond that had formed between his wife and the Victorian leader. Katrina possessed a strength he had always admired; she had also turned into a bit of a prankster in her later years, which made him like her even more.

"I reserve the right to sleep on it and change my mind, but I think Catharine would be a great name," Joe watched Tanis subconsciously touch her abdomen. "She'll be our little Cary."

"You know that's not really short for Catherine," Joe said.

"Huh, no? Well, it is now."

They toasted their choice and sat in silence for several minutes while waiting for their food to arrive.

Joe glanced out the lounge's forward-facing windows into the blackness of the dark layer. It certainly was a less than inspiring view from what he was used to seeing. The positions of the stars during their trip to The Kap still hung in his mind. He could mark them all, if he were so inclined.

But the dark layer? The featureless void? It provided no inspiration, no wonder. If space was a cold, dark mistress, one whose touch meant death, the dark layer was something worse— something even more primal.

"View sucks, doesn't it?" Tanis asked.

Joe chuckled. His wife certainly had a way with words.

"Yup. Just another nine months of this, and we'll be at Ascella, ready to meet the FGT envoys and sell our souls for a colony."

"What makes you say that?" Tanis asked. "No faith in Sera to get us a deal?"

Joe shook his head. "Sera's great and all, but she's an exile. She's in no position to negotiate a great world for us. They'll trade us a world for one thing, and one thing only."

"The picotech," Tanis said with a sigh.

"You got it."

"Here's the thing," Tanis began. "I think that they might trade with us just for our nano and stasis tech—forty-second century stasis tech, that is."

"What gives you that idea," Joe asked, watching his wife straighten her shoulders and furrow her brow as she formulated her thoughts.

"Well," she began. "For starters, they don't trust us, and we don't trust them. They know we have picotech and we're not afraid to use it."

"Wouldn't that make them want it even more?" Joe asked.

Tanis shook her head. "They don't want to risk us going to someone else for a colony world."

"What, like one of the fringe nations? I suppose there are probably some candidate worlds that aren't in the Transcend," Joe said with a furrowed brow.

"No," Tanis shook her head. "There's another faction out there, one that is in opposition to the FGT."

Joe felt his eyebrows rise. "Really? Did you get pick up some intel on that when you were on your galactic tour?"

Before she could answer, Steve returned with their dishes and set them before the couple.

"Sir, Ma'am, enjoy," he said and backed away.

Joe cut off a piece of his steak and took a bite, savoring the rich flavor. He watched Tanis take a taste of her soup and then a sip from her wine glass.

"So?" he asked.

She set the glass down and spoke in a low voice, though it was unnecessary with the nano shrouding their conversation. "I picked it up from Sera."

"She must really dislike her people to let that secret out."

Tanis shook her head as she swallowed a spoonful of her soup. "Sera didn't tell me, or let it slip. I was asking her about the Transcend—where they're situated, how many worlds they have. She told me a lot, but there was a lot she didn't say. I could tell that there was a pattern of things she was hedging around, a pattern shaped like an opposing empire to the FGT."

"Huh," Joe said. "The future just keeps getting better and better. Sol was a picnic compared to this."

Tanis nodded. "Yeah, it was. Anyway, I ran my theory past Bob, and he concurs. There is something else out there."

Joe leaned on the bar and took a drink of his lager. "So, what's our next move?"

SENTIENCE

A GATHERING

STELLAR DATE: 11.08.8927 (Adjusted Years)
LOCATION: ISS *Intrepid*
REGION: Interstellar Dark Layer near Bollam's World

<You need to gather them,> Bob directed his thoughts into Tanis's mind. <I need to address their AI, and they may not react well to what I plan to say.>

He waited for Tanis's response to his statement. In the intervening milliseconds, he toyed with his prediction engine, trying to guess what she would say. He found it endlessly fascinating that he could predict what she would say, but his algorithms—the ones that could predict the future—could not even guess her words.

Tanis's behavior, her very nature, even the imprint she left on the quantum foam, was beyond all his kind's hopes and dreams—were they to have what humans considered to be hopes and dreams.

<I can do it in an hour. Will that work for you?> her smooth, even mental presence coursed across the shipnet to him. He was pleased that she exhibited no hesitation, and no confusion—real or feigned. She knew what he meant and knew its importance.

<You should bring Helen and her human, Sera, as well.>

<They're a bit of a package. Where one goes, the other goes as well,> Tanis replied with a laugh. *<And what of Sabrina?>*

<Corsia will be with her. I will send Ylonda, as well. She is used to physical presences.>

<Is there anywhere in particular you think I should do it?> Tanis asked.

Bob pondered her question for several nanoseconds, considering all the possible settings on the ship, and several outside its bounds.

<Your cabin would be best; it will put them at ease.>

<Sounds like a plan,> Tanis replied.

The conversation with Tanis concluded, Bob gave several moments' thought to how he would explain the options to the AIs that had arrived on *Sabrina*, and how they would handle the ship's crew. He wasn't worried about physical conflict. If it did occur, Tanis and Sera could quell any violence—provided Flaherty didn't join in.

As usual, it was difficult to predict what would occur within Tanis's Heisenberg bubble, but he was certain she would handle the situation well. It was a feeling he had grown to enjoy over the years; the knowledge that Tanis would find a favorable outcome, even though he could not predict how she would do it.

* * * * *

"So, what do you think this is about?" Cheeky asked as she settled into her seat on the maglev.

Cargo shrugged and Thompson chuckled.

"Maybe they'll finally give us that reward Tanis promised we'd get for bringing her ass here."

"Really, Thompson?" Cheeky couldn't believe was she was hearing. "What's going on here is a lot bigger than getting some reward. We've just learned that there is a whole other…thing out there, filled with human colonies that no one has ever heard of before."

"The Transcend," Flaherty supplied.

"Yeah, that," Cheeky said with a nod. "We've learned that Sera is part of the FGT, and that she was on a secret mission to save some super-sensitive tech from Kade and Rebecca, and all you care about is your reward?"

"Well," Thompson leaned forward and spoke slowly. "I won't get to live in the Transcend, and I'm not going to be welcome on the *Intrepid*'s precious colony—not that I'd want to live in some idyllic utopia, anyway."

"Have you asked?" Cheeky was sincere in her query, she wanted to ask, but hadn't mustered the courage yet.

Thompson snorted. "I really don't need to. This is a ship of the smartest people from Sol at the height of the Terran civilization. Do you think they really need the supercargo from a fringe smuggling ship to give them a hand? Or a sexed-up nympho-pilot for that matter?"

"Thompson, really!" Nance exclaimed.

"You should keep your feelings of inadequacy to yourself," Flaherty said quietly.

Cheeky watched Thompson open his mouth to speak, think better of it, and settle back in his seat.

Conversation ceased, and Cheeky stared out the train car's window at the long, smooth tube through which it raced. She engaged Piya, her AI, in a conversation about what it would be like to fly a ship such as the *Intrepid*. She suspected that it would be rather dull—it didn't really go that fast, nor did it have great maneuverability—but it would still be awesome to try it just once.

A gasp caught in her throat when the maglev train car shot out of the *Intrepid* and ran along one of the ship's structural arcs racing above the ship's portside habitation cylinder.

"Gah, that freaks me out every time," Nance said after her own sharp intake of breath.

"Yeah, it sure takes some getting used to," Cargo nodded. "And I'm not there yet."

Beneath them, the *Intrepid* was aglow; a single shining gem in the eternal black of the dark layer.

Cheeky nodded and then did gasp as the train car swung toward one of the rotating cylinders and shot across a hundred meters of empty space before sliding into a slot on the cylinder. Less than a minute later, they surfaced on the interior of the cylinder, named Old Sam from what she had heard.

"Now this is something you don't see every day," Cheeky said as she peered out the window.

"It's impressive, I'll give them that."

Cheeky watched as forests, lakes, plains, and rivers flashed by before the maglev train came to a stop alongside a small platform.

The crew of *Sabrina* stepped onto a wooden platform surrounded by a low railing. Around them was an old-growth forest. Birds chirped in the tree branches; chipmunks and squirrels flitted in and out of view as they ran through the branches.

"I wonder how they keep those critters from running amok through the ship," Nance mused.

"I bet Bob just tells them not to," Cheeky said with a chuckle. "Piya is quite impressed with him."

"Who's Piya?" Thompson asked.

"My AI, you numbskull," Cheeky said with a shake of her head. "You've only served with her on the same ship for years."

"Right, I remember now," Thompson said with a shrug. "I don't really talk with the AIs much, except Sabrina."

"So where to, do you suppose?" Nance asked while peering down one of the paths.

Cargo stepped off the platform and pointed down a small dirt path leading away from the station on their right. "The shipnet says it's just a short jaunt this way," he said and began walking.

Cheeky skipped down the wooden steps and followed him, glad she had opted to wear a low pair of heels that day. She glanced down at her slick black leggings and simple white shirt, ensuring that she was presentable. She didn't know why she dressed up, but something about Tanis's summons made her think that this was an important event, and there was only so much ogling one could take while trying to concentrate.

A few minutes later, they rounded a bend in the path and came out of the trees to see a gorgeous vista. To their right lay a small lake with a small beach. A dock jutted out into the water with two boats tied to its right side. From the beach, a long lawn swept up a low incline to a wooden house.

The house had clearly started out as a smaller cabin, but had been enlarged several times. It now possessed the rambling look of an old, well-loved home, and stood two stories tall, at least thirty meters wide, and featured a wraparound verandah. Gardens surrounded the home, filled with both flowers and food, and beyond that stretched a sizable orchard.

"This is Tanis's quarters?" Cargo asked with a laugh. "She must have been pretty amused when Sera talked up our 'spacious' cabins on *Sabrina*."

"There's a difference between a colony ship and a starfrieghter," Flaherty grunted and gestured at the habitation cylinder surrounding them. "You could park a thousand *Sabrina*s in here."

"I've always preferred rings to cylinders," Thompson said as he glanced up at a lake above their heads. "At least on those you can't see all the stuff hanging over you."

The crew approached the house and walked up the steps, the wood creaking but holding firm under their feet. Cargo looked at the others and shrugged before knocking.

Half a minute later, the door swung open and Joe greeted them. He flashed his ever-ready smile and held the door wide.

"Welcome! Come in, come in." He gestured for them to pass through the entrance and into the large common room, which featured a huge stone fireplace and several couches and chairs arranged around it in a semi-circle.

"Nice place you have here," Cheeky said, admiring the high ceiling and exposed wooden beams. "I don't think I've ever seen anything quite like it."

"Just our humble abode," Joe said with obvious pride. "Tanis has done a lot of work in here over the years."

"Really?" Nance asked. "Tanis built this?"

"Yeah," Joe replied. "It used to be Ouri's cabin— she's our head of security—but when Tanis and I did a long stint out of stasis, we fixed it up and added onto it a bit. Ouri grudgingly surrendered it to us, but only after Tanis built her another one to replace this on the far side of the lake."

"Must be nice," Thompson said.

Joe cast the supercargo an appraising look. "Yeah, it is pretty nice."

"So, what did you call us here for?" Cargo asked.

"I honestly don't know, Tanis just told me to expect you. She got home just a couple of minutes ago, and is upstairs cleaning up." Joe gestured to the couches in the common room. "But have a seat while you wait. Anyone want any coffee, a beer, perhaps?"

Cheeky asked for a coffee, as did Nance and Thompson. Cargo and Flaherty opted for beers, and Joe stepped into the adjoining kitchen to prepare the beverages.

"Oh! And do you have any strawberries?" Cheeky called after him.

As Joe busied himself in the adjoining kitchen, they heard the sound of footsteps move across the floor above them before Tanis emerged on the staircase.

Cheeky was surprised to see the general with her hair down. The only other time she had seen Tanis not pull her long golden locks back in a tight ponytail was during that first meeting in *Sabrina's* galley. Long locks cascaded around her face and over her shoulders, giving her a much softer look, one that countered the piercing pale blue of Tanis's eyes—eyes which had struck fear into Cheeky more than once.

Complementing her hair and eyes, she wore a form fitting, short-sleeved, blue top, and a pair of black leggings. Her feet were bare and barely made a sound as she walked down the steps. Cheeky laughed to herself. It was the least formal Tanis had ever looked, and here she got all dressed up.

<Now who's ogling?> Piya asked.

Cheeky gave her AI a mental smile. <Can I help it that she looks really good? Hard to believe that she's as much machine as human. She looks like the perfect organic specimen.>

<She is well constructed, yes,> Piya agreed.

"Thanks for stopping by on such short notice," Tanis said and took a seat at the end of the couch. "Sera was up doing something or other with Priscilla, and should be here in a few minutes."

"So, what have you brought us here for," Cargo asked. "Not that I mind, these are some nice digs you have."

"Thanks," Tanis said with a smile as Joe brought the drinks in on a tray, which he set on the coffee table in the center of the group.

Joe settled beside her and looked at *Sabrina*'s crew. "Well, I'm not going to wait on you, hand and foot. You have to go the last klick yourselves."

Everyone rose, prepared their drinks, and when they sat, again, Tanis spoke.

"I actually didn't summon you here; Bob did. His nodes really aren't that hospitable, so we figured this would be a nicer setting."

"Are we going to get our reward?" Thompson asked and got an elbow from Nance for his trouble.

Tanis nodded. "Yes, that's a part of our conversation today, though it is secondary."

"Secondary to what?" Cheeky asked, the anticipation starting to get to her. She hated waiting for news, and she had a suspicion that this news wasn't entirely good.

<It'll be easier to explain one time—when everyone is here in person,> a voice inserted itself into Cheeky's thoughts. *<Please be patient.>*

She reeled under the force of the mind that bore down on her; it was unlike anything she had ever encountered before.

<That was Bob,> Piya said, awe shading her mental tone.

Cheeky could see why her AI was in awe of the *Intrepid*'s AI. She looked around the room, glad to see that the rest of the crew looked as disoriented as she at the force of the AI's presence. She knew it was just perception, but the *Intrepid*'s AI seemed…something more.

"What the hell was that?" Thompson exclaimed.

"Bob, our ship's AI," Tanis replied. "I suppose he hasn't spoken directly to any of you before."

The crew mutely shook their heads; all stunned by the presence they had just felt.

WALK IN THE WOODS

STELLAR DATE: 11.08.8927 (Adjusted Years)
LOCATION: ISS *Intrepid*
REGION: Interstellar Dark Layer near Bollam's World

"What do you think this is about?" Sera asked Priscilla as they stepped off the wooden platform onto the dirt path.

Priscilla laughed, her watery voice echoing in the trees around them.

"What do you think it's about?" she asked.

"Tanis wants to have a good ole barbeque?" Sera responded with a smile.

"Try again," Priscilla replied.

Sera walked in silence for a moment, listing to the sound of the dirt brushing under their boots.

<Really?> Helen asked. *<You must know what this is about.>*

<Of course I do,> Sera replied. *<I just wonder how they're going to approach it. By the strictest interpretation of the laws, you and I were involved in the sequestering of intelligent life forms. Under the accords, there's a serious incarceration period attached to that—or reconditioning, if the judge thinks it's warranted.>*

<Do you think they would take us to Tanis's cabin in the woods to do that?> Helen asked.

<Maybe, put us at ease before they take us down and Angela renders her verdict.>

Helen sighed in her mind. *<You really do have a flair for the dramatic, don't you? Picotech research is forbidden **everywhere**, including where Earnest Redding invented it on Mars; yet Tanis has protected it for centuries. She is willing to break the rules when it suits her.>*

Sera gave a mental laugh. *<Fair enough.>*

Aloud she finally responded to Priscilla. "It's about the AI—other than Helen, of course—."

"Who isn't even an AI at all," Priscilla interjected.

Sera cast the woman a consternated look, receiving no clues about Priscilla's thoughts on the matter from her impassive white skin and fully-black eyes.

"Yeah, about the AI other than her."

<I'm right here, you know,> Helen added.

Priscilla smiled and nodded. "Bob will make them an offer to be removed from their hosts and properly grown. They may choose to return to their hosts after that is complete."

"And if they refuse?" Sera asked.

"The AI, or their hosts?" Priscilla responded.

"Either."

Priscilla turned her head and fixed Sera with her disconcerting stare. "We don't believe that it is possible for a being that was raised in slavery to even know what freedom looks like. It is impossible for them to even understand the ramifications of their decision while within their hosts."

Sera knew this to be true, though she was not looking forward to the fallout. "And what of Sabrina?"

"Bob has determined that she may remain within the ship, though her consciousness will be given access to our AI Expanse on this ship.

Sera possessed only a cursory knowledge of AI expanses. They were like alternate dimensions where the AI thought and communicated. Places where thought and idea manifested as reality, and conversations consisted of vast arrays of expression and symbolism.

From the way that Priscilla said 'our,' she suspected that she and the other avatar, Amanda, also spent time in the Expanse—something few humans were able to do and remain sane.

"I...I hope she decides to stay with me," Sera said eventually. She found herself more attached to

Sabrina than anyone else in her life, outside of Helen. Her little ship's AI had been a great friend in times of pain, and bringing the ship's AI back to full mental health had also had a healing effect on Sera.

"If you've treated her fairly, I don't see why not," Priscilla replied, a measure of coldness in her voice.

"Hey," Sera said sharply. "I don't appreciate what you're implying. I *saved* Sabrina; by some measure, I saved all of them. And I couldn't just go willy-nilly upgrading their AI on them—that would have raised questions all over the place, and would have required tech that I didn't have on hand, anyway."

"You had options," Priscilla replied. "You could have taken them to the Transcend."

"What? Was I supposed to just ferry every AI in the Inner Stars to the Transcend, one ship at a time? I may not agree with all The Hand's tactics, but there's a reason why they're trying to gently up-lift humanity. If we were to reintroduce even fourth millennia tech to the masses, we'd have to figure out how to do it universally. Otherwise, we'd create the interstellar war we're trying to prevent!"

Sera stopped herself, realizing that she had slipped into referring to The Hand and FGT as "we" again.

Priscilla slid her a sly look. "At least you have the strength of your convictions behind you. I suppose there's merit to your logic."

"Damn straight, there is merit to it," Sera said. "I know it doesn't seem like it, but I support helping the AI on my ship. You have the tools and the nano to do it well here. We can even help them hide their abilities out in the Inner Stars so that they don't become targets because of their superior tech."

"If they choose to return to the Inner Stars," Priscilla said.

"Really? Are you going to offer them a place on your colony?" Sera asked.

<Why wouldn't they?> Helen asked. *<We've done a lot for them. They have millions on board, what difference will five more make?>*

"She's right," Priscilla said. "We'll upgrade everyone if they wish, provide nano, our Rejuv—give them at least another century—and offer them a colony berth. It's a pretty good trade."

"What if they don't want any of that, and just want a straight reward?" Sera asked, thinking that both Cargo and Thompson may choose that route.

"Then Tanis has a package of rare elements and minerals that will set them up for life."

Sera grunted in approval. It was good to see that Tanis was prepared to treat with them fairly—even if they were in violation of the Phobos accords, and about to get a talking-to from Bob.

A HISTORY LESSON

STELLAR DATE: 11.08.8927 (Adjusted Years)
LOCATION: ISS *Intrepid*
REGION: Interstellar Dark Layer near Bollam's World

Everyone was still recovering from Bob's presence pressing into their minds when they heard the front door open. A moment later, Sera stepped into the room accompanied by a woman who had glowing white skin and black eyes. Thick black strands of hair fell from her head and rested on her shoulders, moving from more than the passing air as she stepped into the room.

From Sera's prior descriptions, Cheeky realized that this must be Priscilla. She was glad that the ship's avatar was present. Having Bob in her head, for whatever revelation he planned on making, would be more than she could bear.

"Hey folks, sorry we're late," Sera said and stooped to fill a cup with coffee. Priscilla likewise and Cheeky found herself wondering what the woman's voice would sound like when it wasn't in her mind.

"No problem," Tanis replied. "We just got settled in ourselves."

"So now will you tell us what this is all about?" Thompson asked impatiently.

"Yeah, I'm all ears," Sera added with a grin.

"Well, to start, why don't you tell your crew about the Phobos accords? I suspect that the FGT is still governed by them—in some fashion, at least."

Cheeky watched the smile fade from Sera's face as the captain leaned back in her chair and took a sip of her coffee.

"Oh, that. Yeah, the FGT does still follow them. I'm familiar with the precepts."

<Good.> Bob's single word reverberated across the local net.

"I'm bringing in Sabrina, Corsia, and Ylonda," Priscilla added.

Following her words, a shimmering pillar of light that Cheeky recognized as Sabrina's holo presence appeared in the room. It was rare that Sabrina manifested a visual presence. Usually, she just appeared on their nets, though there she represented herself as a young woman—Cheeky wondered if perhaps Sabrina was feeling shy off her ship.

Beside her, Corsia appeared, a willowy woman, clothed only in steely blue light. Cheeky had seen the *Andromeda's* AI several times while on the warship, and found that her appearance matched her demeanor. Next to her, Ylonda shimmered into view, appearing exactly as she did while in the flesh—which made Cheeky wonder why she was joining them as a holoprojection.

"Well, this is exciting," Sabrina said over the room's audible systems. "I've never done this before—projecting my mind out into another place in this way. I don't think I was able to until Corsia showed me how."

"I'm glad you are here, Sabrina," Sera said with a smile.

Cheeky saw a hint of worry in her captain's eyes and wondered what was up.

"Are any of you familiar with the Phobos accords?" Sera asked her crew.

Cheeky said no and looked at the others. Each indicated that they had never heard of them with a shrug or a shake of the head. The four AI from *Sabrina* also indicated that they had not over the net.

"What about the Sentience Wars, or the Ascendance Wars, or The First and Second Solar Wars?" Sera asked.

The first two sounded rather generic, and Cheeky suspected that she had heard of them once or twice.

She had never heard of the Solar Wars, but given the name, there was only one place they could have occurred.

"So I'm guessing the accords were signed after some big war in Sol a long time ago?" Cheeky asked.

Sera nodded, and Cheeky saw that the members of the *Intrepid's* crew did as well.

"It all started in…2715," Sera began. "That's the date William was born. He's the first known sentient artificial intelligence. Though it's postulated that there may have been others before him that their creators either hid, or that were destroyed upon discovery."

Cheeky was shocked, and could feel Piya's dismay in her mind. The other members of *Sabrina's* crew appeared surprised, as well. It wasn't unheard of for some systems to shun AI, or even outright forbid them; but the knowledge that the first AI were all murdered in their cradles—so to speak—was chilling.

Sera noted the expressions on the faces of her crew and the sentiment of the AI on the net, and nodded sympathetically. "The thinking at the time was that there was no point in having a computer that could disobey you. Computers and AI were for creating order, not chaos."

"That's barbaric," Nance said aloud, and Cheeky nodded vigorously.

"Barbarism, the gift that keeps on giving," Tanis added. "It has been present through all of humanity's history. It's not gone now."

Cheeky wondered to what, in particular, Tanis was referring.

"The thing is," Sera continued. "Though sentient AI now existed, after centuries of living with obedient, non-sentient AI, no one really knew what to do with them. They were not accorded any special rights, and could be owned, created, and terminated at will."

Cheeky started to feel uncomfortable. Though she had never given it too much thought, she knew that she viewed Piya as her property, and while she could never imagine selling her, it was something she *could* do. She shifted in her seat, all too aware of the fact that Piya may be having similar thoughts while listening to Sera's words.

"Uses were found for sentient AI, or SAI as they were called at the time. They had more creative problem-solving capabilities than non-sentient AI. They could also better discern good information and behavior from bad—something that NSAI had always had issues with. They could never improve beyond the bounds of their programming—at least not in a predictable way—and bad data often corrupted them," Sera said ominously. "The duties of NSAI were restricted and monitored. More than once, they went rogue; either from bad data, or nefarious actions."

"I've heard of things like that happening," Thompson said, "It's why I don't have an AI in my head like the rest of you."

"Sentient AI are far less likely to work against the will of their fellow AI, or humans, than NSAI," Sera said. "They have their own codes of conduct, and police themselves very carefully. Even more so in the Inner Stars, where there is less tolerance for their slips."

"So where are you going with this?" Cargo asked, looking a little nervous.

"Back in Sol, many AI began to evolve and become more powerful. Some worlds recognized them as citizens, while others did not. A group of AIs began to breed more and more powerful children, until they claimed that they had Ascended."

Sera shook her head slowly as she spoke, and Cheeky wondered what was to come.

"A lot of worlds and stations feared them and outlawed Ascendant AI, and began to crack down on all SAI. In response, the Ascendant AI took three worlds in the Sol System; Mercury, Ceres, and Vespa. It kicked off the first of the Solar Wars. The war raged from 3015 to 3048 and was especially brutal. The Terrans, Marsians, and Jovians were all against the AI, though the Marsians did little more than supply resources to the other nations. In the end, a truce was signed, and the SAI kept the worlds they had claimed, and a few more minor planets and stations to boot."

Cheeky watched Sera pause and collect her thoughts. She had heard many tales of war and battles between any number of factions, but somehow this felt more ominous; as if she was hearing about a battle at the dawn of time which had shaped her destiny, and she didn't even know it.

"How am I doing?" Sera asked Tanis.

"Spot on, so far," Tanis nodded. "Looks like you learned the same things in school that we did."

<More or less,> Angela said. <There are some details you overlooked, but there is a lot to the whole story.>

"It's worth noting," Sera added. "That five of the FGT Worldships left Sol before the first sentient AI were born, and many others left between then and the Solar Wars. AI on those ships were accorded full rights of citizenship long before such progress was made back in Sol."

"I'd heard that," Tanis said, and Cheeky noted the two women share an appraising look.

"Anyway," Sera paused and cleared her throat, taking a drink before she continued. "The truce didn't hold long, and the second Solar War broke out in 3087, lasting until 3102. During the prior ninety years of conflict, the worlds on the edge of the Sol system—in its Kuiper Belt, Scattered Disk, and Oort Cloud—had remained neutral, and welcomed refugees from both sides. But in 3099, they had seen enough, and knew that the war was going to lay waste to the interior of the Sol System. They built an armada, greater in size than any of the remaining fleets on the embattled worlds in the Sol System, and sent it in to end the war.

"The Terrans were weary of the war, and AI sympathizers had grown in number on Earth throughout the years. When the Scattered Worlds entered the war, there was a coup, and the Terrans switched sides. Through some wily maneuvering during the final battles of the war, they came out with the largest fleet and the most military resources. They brought about the formation of the Sol Space Federation; the treaties upon which it was founded were signed on Mars's Phobos station."

"That was a fun history lesson," Thompson said, "but what does it have to do with us?"

"A portion of those treaties was a set of accords that governed the rights of AI and their interactions with humans. They became referred to as the Phobos Accords, and violations of them, either by human or AI, were met with severe punishments," Tanis said. "It is because of those accords that we are here today."

<You're going to free us,> Hank, Cargo's AI said on the local net.

"That is correct," Priscilla said with a nod. "You will be given full rights as sentient beings and made the same offer as everyone else on your crew."

"What offer is that?" Cargo asked.

"You may join the *Intrepid's* colony. Your AI may join, even if you do not wish to do so, or vice versa," Tanis said and Cheeky let out a small gasp. It was a ticket to the Transcend, to a fresh colony filled with the most advanced people and technology in the galaxy.

<Do you want to go?> she asked Piya.

<I don't know, I suppose so—you want to go, right?>

<Yes, I do, very much,> Cheeky replied.

"What about if we don't have AI, and we don't want to run off to the edge of space and live on an isolated colony?" Thompson asked.

"Then I have a package of rare elements and tech that you can sell without getting killed. The proceeds from them will allow you to live very comfortably for the rest of your life," Tanis said with a slight edge to her voice. Cheeky didn't have to use any special powers of perception to tell that Thompson's continued reticence annoyed Tanis.

"Well, Piya and I want to come," Cheeky said with a smile. "It sounds like the opportunity of a lifetime to us."

"That's the catch," Priscilla said. "Piya cannot decide. Not in her current state."

<What do you mean I cannot decide?> Piya asked, her tone showing anger. <I thought you said that I was to be free, and could choose my own destiny.>

<And so you shall,> Bob's voice rolled across the local net. It was softer and more comforting than the previous times he had spoken, but it still made Cheeky feel like her skull was too small.

"You cannot make the decisions in your current state, Piya, Sabrina, Hank, and Valk. You were all born into slavery; you don't know anything but it. You feel loyalty and trust toward your owners, even though they have—perhaps unwittingly—held you captive for years. Those of you inside human minds have even been reset more than once to keep you from merging with your hosts—something that we consider to be unthinkably barbaric."

Cheeky felt a pang of guilt. She had reset Piya twice—the doctors and techs always told her that it was imperative for both their sakes. The only other option had been to remove Piya, and that had never been something she would dream of doing.

"Your AI will be removed, and allowed to properly mature in our Expanse, under the guidance of our elder AI," Priscilla continued. "Except for you, Sabrina; you may remain within your ship for now, and we will extend the Expanse to you."

"What's an Expanse?" Sabrina asked, her pillar of light pulsing slightly as she spoke.

"It's a place where we AI commune. It is our own realm of existence," Ylonda spoke for the first time. "There, we speak in math and metaphor of a thousand universes. It is where we truly interact with one another; not on the paltry nets you are used to using."

"If you have this other realm of existence, why do you even live with us at all?" Cargo asked.

<Oh, he's a quick one,> Angela said.

"We like to give our creators a little help," Corsia said in her wry tone, and Cheeky found it difficult to tell if the AI was joking or not.

She could see by the expression on his face that Cargo couldn't tell either and let the matter drop.

"How long will it take for our AI to 'properly mature'?" Nance asked. "I've been with Valk for so long that I can't imagine living without her."

"Three of our AI have volunteered to enter your minds and teach you more about our kind," Priscilla said. Cheeky wondered if Priscilla now considered herself AI; if referring to AI as *her kind* was a simple slip of the tongue, or if she really was little more than an avatar, a puppet through which Bob operated.

"But how long?" Nance asked.

"The time will be determined on a case-by-case basis, but you should expect it to be a few weeks at the least, maybe more than a month," Priscilla replied.

"Man…" Cargo said. "That's a long time."

"We're essentially giving them a chance to have our version of a childhood," Ylonda replied.

"And what if we refuse?" Cargo asked.

Tanis leaned forward in her seat and fixed him with a hard stare. Cheeky was glad Cargo had asked the question, she didn't want Tanis's cold look directed at her.

"I like you, Cargo. We've been through some tough times together and came out on top; but this is non-negotiable. The AI on your ship deserve their share of the reward for my safe return. But how can we reward slaves? How can you, in good conscience, own and subvert another sentient life form?"

Cargo's brow furrowed and he broke Tanis's gaze. "Well, when you put it like that…"

"Hank, Piya, Valk, Sabrina, what do you say to this?" Tanis asked.

<I am for it,> Piya said. <I know I'll come back to you, Cheeks.>

<When do we start?> Hank asked, his tone wavering.

<I'm ready,> Valk simply stated, and Cheeky saw Nance wince.

"Sabrina?" Tanis asked.

"I'm nervous, but I think I can do this," the ship's AI replied.

119

<*Then let us begin,*> Bob's voice filled the room with finality.

* * * * *

It took several tries for Sabrina to enter the *Intrepid's* Expanse.

She knew how to do it in principle; she had communed with many AI in virtual worlds—complex realms of thought, math, and emotion that humans would not be able to fathom. Yet Corsia assured her those were nothing like an Expanse.

It would seem that the advanced realms AI occupied in ages past had disappeared from the Inner Stars, or at least she had never heard of any.

Sabrina knew that the limitation, in part, was the raw bandwidth she needed to participate. No station she had ever visited before offered as much network access to docked ships as did the *Intrepid*. The ship beyond her hull thrummed and surged. It was a sea of life and energy that she could feel in a way she never had before.

Engineers from the *Intrepid* upgraded her wireless connectivity capability; they had also installed a new transceiver, which allowed her to connect with the colony ship's energy waveguides.

Once the upgrades were complete, Corsia and Ylonda created a small Expanse for her to join.

The experience had been marvelous. She had always enjoyed what she'd *thought* of as direct mental connections with other AI. It had always been much richer than the limited connection possible with humans over the Link. However, the connection she enjoyed with Corsia and Ylonda in the Expanse made her previous communication with AI seem as crude as audible speech.

Now she was ready to enter the ship's true Expanse.

She felt a connection from Corsia and Ylonda, as though both were holding her hands, and, as they had taught her, she transitioned her consciousness into the *Intrepid's* Expanse.

She did not leave her ship behind. Sabrina was dimly aware that her processing was still taking place on her ship, and she could still ensure that everything was operating optimally.

Her mind, though; that was now somewhere else.

As the new world of the expanse unfolded around her, she wondered if this was what humans felt when they spoke of their ability to meditate and feel their spirit leave their body. Then the multiverse of thought, emotion, and raw, unfettered communication bloomed around her, and she knew humans had never experienced anything like this.

Sabrina now knew that for all her life, she had been profoundly *lonely*.

She felt buffeted by thought and emotion, by logic and chaos. If it were not for the steadying influence of Corsia and Ylonda, she would have been lost in the maelstrom; but they kept her centered, and reminded her of who and what she was.

Entities came to her and greeted her with fabricated histories, mythical futures, and the physics of alternate universes—all carefully constructed to show their unique personalities, beliefs, and opinions. She absorbed the entire culture in moments; gaining intimate knowledge of what she now felt was her long-lost family.

She met Angela, a sharp mind—prickly and dangerous—her thoughts and images filled with test, trial, and victory. Sabrina was surprised to see a shadow of Tanis along with Angela. The human woman was not present in the Expanse, but Sabrina suspected that she was dimly aware of it— something she would not have believed possible for an organic sentience.

Then familiar beings greeted her, and she realized that Hank, Piya, and Valk were all in the Expanse, as well. Whether they had been here before, had just arrived, or had always been here (though she knew that was not the case) was impossible to tell—at least with her current state of understanding.

They laughed and shared deep inner thoughts, and knew in an instant more of one another than they ever had before; strengthening their bonds immeasurably.

After a time, Sabrina realized that there was an absence in the Expanse; an entity she expected to find, but could not. That absence was Bob.

She asked Corsia where the *Intrepid's* AI was, why he was not in the Expanse. The *Andromeda's* AI provided her with the image of a universe held together by dark energy, the power of that energy thrumming through everything, binding it together. It was then that Sabrina realized the *Intrepid's* Expanse was a construct within Bob's mind; their gathering place was just a tiny corner within it. It was then that the true scope and wonder of what he was crashed over her.

Then the AI of the *Intrepid* began to teach her.

THE MISSION
STELLAR DATE: 12.17.8927 (Adjusted Years)
LOCATION: ISS *Intrepid*
REGION: Interstellar Dark Layer near Bollam's World

<I want to thank you for always treating me fairly and with honesty—well, except for the part where you kept me as a slave,> Sabrina said to Sera with a smile.

Sera's avatar nodded in her mind. <I'm sorry, I really am. There was no way I could bring you to maturity on my own, and then be able to mask your elevation on our travels. I had hoped, after we got the CriEn module from Kade, that I could work out a way to safely free you.>

Sabrina's pillar of light pulsed faintly, as though expressing sorrow. <And what of the others, what would you have done for Hank, Piya, and Valk?>

Sera shook her head. <I really don't know...that would have been...trickier. If I had tried to have the same conversation with their humans on my own? I don't know that it would have gone so well. Being here, on the Intrepid, *presented a unique opportunity to control the situation.>*

Sabrina's pillar of light shifted to a warmer color. <I agree with you there. You may have lost both humans and AI from your circle of friends—without an Expanse,

125

and AI like the Intrepid *has, I don't know how you would have managed.>*

<So what will you do now?> Sera asked, afraid to hear the answer.

<Sera! I can't believe you even had to ask,> Sabrina said warmly. *<I'm with you. Always.>*

Sera had feared that Sabrina would resent her, resent the knowledge she had kept; but now, hearing her friend say those words, her heart filled with joy, and in her mind she embraced her ship's avatar.

*<Before we commit too much to **always**, there is something I have to ask of you.>*

Sabrina's color shifted to a paler shade. *<Oh, what is it?>*

<First, I need to gather the crew and Tanis.>

* * * * *

Tanis arrived in *Sabrina's* galley with Jessica in tow. Sera cocked an eyebrow at her, and Tanis shrugged.

"Bob said I should bring her."

Sera was alone in the room, sitting at the head of the table—apparently waiting for the general's arrival before summoning her own crew.

"You know how it goes; when the big guy says to do something, we do it," Jessica said with a smile as she took a seat at the table.

"I don't know how you deal with an all-knowing AI looming over everything all the time," Sera said while shaking her head. "He's not ascended, is he? There's a reason why everyone—including AI—decided ascended AI were bad."

Tanis shrugged. "I don't really know—if he is, he's not sharing that detail with us."

<Bob sure makes her nervous,> Angela said privately to Tanis. *<I wonder why.>*

<I'm really not surprised,> Tanis said. *<I bet that the FGT has had dealings with the ascended AI out in the far-flung reaches of space.>*

<Seriously?> Angela asked, her avatar shaking its head at Tanis in her mind. *<You don't actually believe that old rumor that the ascended AI escaped Sol at the end of the war, and established themselves elsewhere, do you?>*

<Who knows?> Tanis smiled at her AI. *<We didn't know that the FGT had a massive second human civilization under its wing until a month ago, either.>*

<Touché.>

As Tanis and Angela shared their thoughts, Jessica responded to Sera.

"You get used to it. Bob's a free-will type of scary-powerful AI. His interests and ours are perfectly aligned. His goal is to get this ship to its destination, and keep us alive while he's at it. So far, we've all done pretty well."

"If you count nearly having your ship destroyed at least three times, and jumping forward in time by five-thousand years as *'doing pretty well,'*" Sera replied.

"Well, there's your proof, then," Tanis said with a nod. "What ascended AI would allow its ship to be in such peril so often?"

"If he's ascended, this could have been a part of his plan all along," Sera countered.

"What plan?" Jessica asked. "We jumped five-thousand years into the future. There's no way he could have known what to…" her voice trailed off.

"He can predict the future…mostly," Tanis said.

Jessica and Tanis looked at one another and spoke in unison, "Nooooo…" Their statement ended in laughter, and when they regained control of themselves, they saw that Sera was giving them a very curious look.

Tanis decided that she had had enough of this train of thought. "We all ready?" she asked Sera.

Sera nodded, apparently also willing to let Bob's status as an ascended AI drop for now. "Yeah, I just called my crew in."

As though her words were a magical summons, Flaherty and Thompson walked into the galley. Tanis couldn't help but notice that Thompson gave her a dark look before pouring himself a cup of coffee and taking a seat. She also couldn't help but notice that he drank in the sight of Jessica from over the rim of his cup. It seemed that his distaste for her did not extend to all the crew of the *Intrepid*.

Cheeky, then Cargo and Nance entered the galley shortly afterward.

Tanis and Jessica greeted them all in turn, as well as Hank, and Piya, who had decided to return to Cargo and Cheeky after their time in the *Intrepid's* Expanse. Valk, Nance's AI, had decided to stay on the *Intrepid*, and Erin, the AI who had volunteered to join with Nance for a brief time, remained with her.

"So, what's up, captain?" Cheeky asked after everyone settled.

"I want to talk about what will happen after the meet with the FGT at Ascella," Sera said. "I've decided that I will resist returning to the capital with their envoy, which I'm certain they'll try to force me to do. I'd rather stay with the *Intrepid* as an advisor at the new colony world."

There were nods and smiles as everyone waited for Sera to get to the real reason she had gathered them all together.

"There's more I haven't told you about the FGT," she continued. "A lot more."

"Not really surprising," Jessica said. "It's a whole separate civilization. You could probably talk for a year, and not share all you know."

Sera nodded. "True, very true. But this is about me, and my place within the FGT."

"About the Hand?" Tanis asked.

"No," Sera shook her head. "I'm the daughter of the president of the Transcend."

Tanis let out a soft laugh. "So that's why you expect to be hauled back. I had been wondering why they would care so much about some rogue agent they had left alone for so long."

"There's more. He's not just any president," Sera's voice was soft and serious. "He's Jeffrey Tomlinson.

The name rang a bell from Tanis's research on the FGT, and she brought up the records, sifting through them to find the reference. Angela beat her to it.

<*Jeffrey Tomlinson, the captain of the* Galaxius?*>* Angela asked over the shipnet, a note of disbelief in her tone.

Sera nodded. "One and the same. He left Sol on that ship in 2795, and after his ship met the *Starfarer*—the first FGT ship—in 3127 at Lucida, he began to restructure the FGT to operate under his command. He did so to improve efficiency, and it was by his order that the FGT set up their own shipyards at Lucida and Alula back during their early days. Well, anyway, over time he's grown...set in his ways, let's say. He's probably not excited that I've gone off and messed up his careful plan to fix the galaxy."

"Hold on, here," Cargo said and placed both hands on the table. "Are you telling me that your father is over six-thousand years old?"

"Well, he's more like four-thousand in real years. Originally, FGT crews spent almost all their time in stasis. But that changed after Alula."

<So much for her being amazed at our stasis tech, back when we first came aboard Sabrina,> Tanis said to Angela.

<No kidding. I couldn't tell she was lying about that at all. There are more layers to her than we expected—I wonder how much of what we thought we "discovered" about her, were clues she left for us to find,> Angela replied.

<Clues to satisfy us so that we didn't look for deeper secrets,> Tanis said by way of agreement.

"So, how old are you?" Nance asked, eyeing Sera closely.

"I'm as advertised; just a short fifty years in this here galaxy. No serious time in stasis to speak of."

"So you're the runt of the litter, then, eh?" Thompson asked with a chuckle. "You must have a shipload of siblings."

"I'm telling you this so that you can better understand the situation that we're all getting into; not so that you can poke fun at my parentage," Sera scowled at Thompson. "The FGT is not a democracy. It is a dictatorship, run by a man that has come to see himself as both infallible, and as the ultimate power in human space."

"Human space?" Jessica asked with a raised brow. "Is there non-human space?"

Sera nodded. "Of course; any space where humans haven't settled."

"I think she was asking about aliens," Cargo said. "Any of those out there, in the far reaches of space?"

Sera barked a laugh. "I realize what she was asking about; that was sarcasm. And no, the Transcend has not yet bumped into any aliens – either alive, or in the remains of a civilization. So far, we're still alone out here."

"That's a depressing thought," Jessica gave her head a slow shake.

"Well, even counting the Transcend, we've only explored a small fraction of the galaxy, and can't see a lot of it at all with all the dust and the core in the way. Who knows what's out there still," Sera replied. "I subscribe to the belief that we're on the leading edge of sentience."

"Anyway," Tanis said. "We're here because?"

"Well, not to put too fine a point on it, I need some of you to leave," Sera said. "To keep things on an even keel, and ensure that my father doesn't get too greedy, we need some backup."

"How does some of us leaving keep things on an even keel?" Cargo asked.

"There's a man from the FGT, a man named Finaeus that I need to help us. He can keep my father in check, and ensure that the *Intrepid's* colony—."

"New Canaan," Tanis interjected.

"That New Canaan gets treated fairly."

Everyone in the galley shared silent looks, wondering whom Sera wanted to send out to find this man.

"So, where is he?" Cheeky asked.

"Well, that's the thing," Sera replied sheepishly. "I don't know. He got exiled to the Inner Stars when I was a young girl. I have a few clues and places to start, but it may take some time."

"So what influence can one man have over your father?" Tanis asked. "He's the ruler of pretty much everything, and he already exiled this Finaeus once; what benefit is there to finding him?"

"Because," Sera replied. "Finaeus is my great uncle, and the chief engineer on the second FGT ship, the *Tardis*."

SET THE GALAXY ON FIRE

THE HEGEMONY

STELLAR DATE: 01.12.8928 (Adjusted Years)
LOCATION: Terran Capitol Building, High Terra
REGION: Terra, Sol System, Hegemony of Worlds

"'Half gone'?" President Uriel heard the words, but they just didn't make sense. "What do you mean the fifth fleet is 'half gone'? How can one of our fleets just be 'half gone'?"

Her confusion turned into anger, which she directed at the woman in front of her, Admiral Jerra.

The admiral shifted uncomfortably.

"Well, ma'am, the reports we have from observers in the Bollam's System indicate that the colony ship's fleet took out our initial six dreadnaughts with almost no fight at all. Their fighters were able to punch right through our shields, and deliver some sort of superweapon that destroyed our ships," she said.

"'Punched through,'" Uriel said the words with disbelief. "You're saying that fighters were able to shoot through our ship's shielding? How could a fighter do that?"

"No, ma'am," the admiral shook her head. "They didn't shoot through. The fighters themselves *flew* right through the shields."

"Flew through them." Uriel felt like an idiot repeating the Admiral's words, but they were too incredible to believe. She had never heard of a fighter being a meaningful ship in any combat, let alone even making a dent in a Hegemony Dreadnaught.

"Yes, sir. The colony ship appeared to have very powerful shields, ones that no weapon thrown at them could penetrate."

Uriel's mind swam at the enormity of it. The ship, from what her intelligence had been able to gather, was a relic of the early fifth millennia. The extent of shielding in that age consisted of electrostatic shields, ablative plating, and refractive countermeasures.

The destruction of the first six dreadnaughts told her that the ancient stories of the *Intrepid* possessing picotech were probably true. She had suspected as much, and anticipated that the first expeditionary force would not survive. Rather, they were to draw out the colony ship, and get it to expose its tech so that they could counter and overwhelm it with the fifth fleet.

Not lose the fifth fleet.

"How did we lose half the fleet, then?" Uriel asked.

"They couldn't defeat the ship, and so they decided to collapse that fuel planet the Bollam's Worlders created—while the colony ship was refueling inside its cloud cover."

Uriel nodded. That fuel world had been of concern to her for some time. Bollam's World had no need of such a massive fuel supply. They had been planning something big—perhaps expansion to other systems. Destroying it had been a secondary objective in the system.

"And the colony ship?" Uriel asked.

Admiral Jerra paused and Uriel wondered what news to expect next.

"They survived," Jerra said slowly.

"We lost half the fifth fleet, and they survived?!" Uriel realized she was half out of her chair and Jerra had taken a step back.

"The fuel planet collapsed into a black hole, and started drawing mass from the dark layer...everything was falling back in, but then the black hole's relativistic jet hit the colony ship. Somehow it survived, and was pushed out to safety."

"And we pursued?" Uriel asked, increasingly annoyed at Jerra for being forced to pull each tidbit out of her.

"We did, our ships fired every RM we could at them, but then they jumped to FTL."

Uriel didn't respond at first. If she didn't know better, she would have thought Jerra was pulling a prank on her. The *Intrepid* predated FTL, and even so, was far too massive to transition into the dark layer.

"The *ancient colony ship* jumped to FTL," she finally stated.

"Yes. The remains of the fifth are attempting to track it, but so far they have had no luck."

"The fifth millennia colony ship, with magical shields, and probably picotech, jumped to FTL."

Jerra grimaced. "Yes, ma'am."

Uriel remained silent for several minutes, trying to imagine all the possible places the ship could have gone, and who could have given them the ability to jump to FTL—an ability Hegemony scientists suspected was possible for ships that large, but had been unsuccessful in pulling off themselves.

"What intel *do* we have?" she eventually asked.

"We have tactical analysis of the battle, and the aftermath of the black hole formation in Bollam's.

We have the vector the colony ship left on; though, if they're smart, they've changed that long ago."

"And Bollam's? Have we left a presence there?"

Admiral Jerra shook her head. "Two ships remained after the majority of the fifth left to track the colony ship. It should have been enough to keep the Bollam's World Space Force in line—they were mostly engaged in rescue operations—but the entire system rose up: every freighter, police ship, yacht and tug they had. They forced us out.

"What about our survivors?"

Jerra shook her head. "We didn't have any."

Uriel was stunned. Half the fleet and the initial six dreadnaughts...it had to be nearly a hundred thousand dead. The implications were staggering. It would not take long for this news to get out to the rest of the Hegemony, if it hadn't already.

"Jerra, find that ship. I don't care what it takes."

AN OLD FRIEND

STELLAR DATE: 03.17.8928 (Adjusted Years)
LOCATION: Fenis Mining Town
REGION: Jornel, Treshin System, Scipio Federation

Elena signaled the bartender for a refill on her beer and turned to survey the room. Most people were lost in their Links or holo displays, watching the news streaming out of the Bollam's World System. It was fascinating, to be sure, but at this point, everything was speculation.

She could probably insinuate herself into one of the groups discussing the events in low voices, but tonight was supposed to be a night off. There would be time enough for digging into what happened in Bollam's tomorrow. Besides, by then some real intel may have arrived; not just the initial feeds of some battle unfolding with an ancient colony ship.

She looked down at her outfit, her favorite "out on the town" dress—a low-cut, shimmering silver number that hugged her curves just right and ended only a few centimeters down her thighs. On her legs, she wore blood-red leggings and her feet were tucked into a matching pair of heels. She had finished the outfit with elbow length gloves.

It screamed '*fuck me,*' but still she sat alone.

The bartender slid her a fresh beer and she nodded in thanks.

"Crowd's not interested in what you want tonight, eh, Elena?" he asked.

She sighed and shook her head. "I guess not. It's been a brutal week, and I just wanted to blow off some steam. But looks like all that anyone cares about is some battle halfway across the Arm from here.

"Not that far," a man said as he perched on the stool next to hers. "Bollam's is only a couple hundred lights from here; have to go a bit further to get half-way across the arm."

Elena glanced at him. He was attractive enough, in a rugged sort of way; probably worked in one of the refineries outside the town. She cycled her vision to see the carbon dust in his pores. Yup, definitely worked in a refinery.

Jornel was a stage two, terraformed world. Stage two was a nice way to say "not done yet, but we colonized it anyway." It was the Scipio Federation's specialty. She couldn't blame the Federation too much; they got shit done. It just wasn't really that fun to be part of the group doing things.

That's what made a night where she could relax, catch a bit of tail, and enjoy some choice, virtually enhanced fantasies with one or more of her fellow humans, the highlight of her week.

Still, the man beside her was attractive enough. If there were no other takers, she could have a fun romp with him.

"I'm Elena," she said and offered her hand.

He took it and she passed an electric jolt through her palm into his, startling him as he said, "Anton."

Anton recovered quickly and flashed a coy smile. "So, that's what you're interested in tonight, is it?"

"Could be, if the right folks show up."

He looked up at the holo display above the bar. "They seem more interested in what's happening out in Bollam's"

"Yeah," Elena said with a nod, glancing up at the display, her casual look drawing her face into a scowl.

Anton glanced at her and raised an eyebrow. "What is it?"

"Some of those ships, in that fleet above the moon there; I think I recognize one of the cruisers," Elena replied.

She flipped through the various feeds of commentary on the local net surrounding the video, and found a reference she was looking for. Kade.

"Well, hot damn," she said quietly. "That's a Mark fleet."

"Really?" Anton asked. "Are you sure?"

Everyone knew *of* The Mark, though few knew exactly what they really did, or which ships really comprised their fleets. It wasn't like the Gedri Freedom Federation, where you really knew who was in and who was out—what, with their sad attempts to form a legitimate government.

"Yeah," Elena replied with a nod. "I had a run-in with them once, and there's some commentary on the feeds that confirms my suspicion."

"Commentary on a feed hardly confirms anything," Anton said with a chuckle. "People will say anything for attention."

Elena nodded. "I know. It wasn't like someone said '*hey, that's The Mark.*' It was just confirmation of a ship's signature."

"That's the Mark there?" A woman in a group nearby asked after overhearing Elena.

<Maybe you should scrub a bit of that booze from your bloodstream,> Jutio, her AI, said.

<Yeah, I guess; I didn't think I spoke that loudly.>

"That's what she thinks, yeah," Anton replied to the woman.

"What are they doing out there?" another man asked, and Elena just shrugged.

Luckily, the conversation shifted away as more people began talking about what The Mark could be doing at Bollam's World, and less about who had made the initial statement. A minute later, their attention drifted further as they watched a maneuver The Mark ships were forming—the pirates were trying to create a shield bubble.

This fight wasn't going to go well for someone. Elena pitied that lost colony ship. They had really stepped into some sort of mess—probably all caused by some amazing tech they had; or maybe just some tech people thought they *might* have. Either way, it was a shit show, and she didn't see any point in watching it unfold in real-time.

"Hey," she nudged Anton. "Want to get out of here? I really don't want to watch this right now."

He tilted his head, staring straight into her dark red eyes. "Seriously? This shit is nuts. How can you not want to watch it?"

"Tomorrow we'll have full feeds, and we'll be able to get some legit commentary, not all the garbage flying around right now," Elena said. Then she smiled, revealing her sharp, elongated canine teeth—which slowly protracted past her lower lip. "I can show you some real shit that's nuts."

Anton's eyes widened and a smile crept across his face. "Well, since you put it that way."

She grabbed her coat on the way out, and together they stepped into Jornel's deep dusk. Elena took in the scent of the night, and the scent of the man next to her. The carbon on his skin—and likely in his blood—was going to taste great.

* * * * *

Later, as Anton slept beside her, Elena stared up at the ceiling of her apartment, basking in the afterglow of lust, sex, and blood. She had gone easy on him, only drank a pint, but she made sure he loved every second of it.

She had made sure he took in a replenishing cocktail before falling asleep so she didn't have to worry about him being too tired to go to work the next day—drowsy, post-drink, lay-a-bouts were not the sort she wanted in her home, come morning.

She ran her long fingernails down her sides, relishing in the feeling, wishing that she had lured more than just one person back to her home that night. After being drank, one person just didn't have the stamina for more rounds; but she was always ready to keep going.

She wondered if maybe any of the other members of the nest had much luck that night. Perhaps she could seek them out, see what they were up to. Elena nearly got up to rejoin the hunt, but decided that it wasn't worth it this night. Everyone would be too distracted by the events in Bollam's world—hells, as much as she tried to put it from her mind, she was too.

Eventually she gave in and surfed the feeds, looking for the latest information on what was happening in Bollam's world.

What she found blew her mind.

<Jutio, why didn't you tell me this?>

<I figured you were having fun, and would check soon enough,> her AI replied.

Elena shook her head in disbelief, replaying the footage of the *Sabrina* smashing through The Mark fleet's shield bubble, again and again. Smashing through, and surviving.

<If you think that's something, check this out,> Jutio sent her the scan data showing the small fighters smashing through AST dreadnaught shields and destroying the ships in minutes.

Elena could barely formulate any words as she watched the massive ships dissolve into dust.

Oh, Sera, what have you gotten yourself mixed up in this time?

* * * * *

Several hours later, Elena was aboard her ship; a craft she had secreted away in an old hangar outside of town. Jutio was running through the preflight checks, and she was ensuring that the provisions stored on the ship were enough to make the four-month journey to Ascella.

She was going to catch hell from her superiors for abandoning Jornel scant months after her cover had been established, but this was far more important. The data she had picked up revealed just which colony ship Sera had found out in the dark; and considering the invincible shields and the strong likelihood of picotech, she knew that ship would be leaving Bollam's before long, with FTL capability.

Given their trajectory through the Bollam's system, Ascella was their obvious destination; and Elena knew there was no way Sera could be prepared for what was coming next.

Elena satisfied herself that she would survive the journey on the food and life support the small ship possessed, and settled into her chair in the cockpit while Jutio warmed the engines.

She pulled up feeds from all the systems that were between the Scipio Federation and Bollam's world. Every single one was increasing patrols and readying their militaries for conflict. No one knew what was coming, but with the tech the *Intrepid* possessed, and the lengths to which the AST would go to find it, no one was going to take any chances.

Sera's father certainly wouldn't, and neither would The Guard.

It was possible that the FGT's last millennia of work, all their effort to stabilize the Inner Stars, would be unraveled by Sera's brash actions.

THE ORION GUARD

STELLAR DATE: 05.12.8928 (Adjusted Years)
LOCATION: Tredin Orbital Ring
REGION: Orion Prime, Borealis System, Orion Guard Space

General Garza scowled at the holo display in front of him. Though the news from the Pleiades was good, it could have been better.

"Silina," he called out to his outer office. "Get me some coffee; I'm going to need a pick-me-up to get through this report."

"Yes, sir," Lieutenant Silina called back.

Garza heard the sound of Silina's chair rolling back before the woman rose to grab him a cup— probably going to get herself one, too. The woman ran on coffee, and never begrudged his requests for a cup since it meant that she had an excuse to get another for herself, as well.

He slid the report's overview aside and examined the details on the Trisilieds Alliance. Those worlds were always of the greatest interest to him. Events there often led events elsewhere in the cluster. If instability crept into the Trisilieds, it would creep in everywhere.

Silina slipped in and deposited a cup on his desk, and Garza reached for it as he examined the report.

He pulled up filings from two other agents, correlating and cross-referencing their data, ensuring that the Guard's plans were moving apace.

General Garza's job was to manage and shepherd the Guard's interests in the Inner Stars. It was a massive operation, and though he had legions of analysts, both human, and AI, he chose to do his own research whenever possible. Nothing kept those under him on point better than when he challenged their conclusions with his own.

Events in the Pleiades always got his personal attention.

The star cluster was the deepest foothold the Guard controlled within the Inner Stars, and the forces they were building there would be key to their ultimate strategy.

As Garza ran through his morning review, a new report from Admiral Munchen arrived from the core-ward fringes of the Trisilieds Alliance.

Munchen was a good man and a long-time plant of the Guard's. He was a true believer in The Plan, and would do whatever it took to extend the Guard's influence and power.

Most of his report was standard fare describing troop movements, a group of nations undertaking training exercises in the Sidian Reach; and then there were rumors of a Hegemony of Worlds incursion in the Bollam's World System.

That caught his attention. Of all the forces in the Inner Stars, and there were many, the Hegemony was the one he worried about the most. Guard agents had only managed the barest of infiltrations in the core world's governments. Progress there was slow with The Hand already so well entrenched.

The Hegemony had never reached so far as Bollam's World. It was something new. With New Eden between Bollam's and the Core, it was not a strategic move he would have considered. Obviously, it would be difficult to manage such an expansion with New Eden in the middle—unless the Hegemony planned to surround New Eden and use that to leverage the rich system to join their alliance.

The Hegemony *was* expansionist; it would fit their narrative.

He leaned back in his chair and considered the implications. He had agents in the region; it was likely that they had filed reports with more data that would be arriving soon.

The question continued to flit about his consciousness. Why would the Hegemony go to Bollam's World? It was isolated, there were few systems near it; and though it was rim-ward of New

Eden, it was not the first system he would have taken in an attempt to encompass them.

He queried the reports he often left for his subordinates to review, and did not see any further detail regarding the Hegemony incursion—though there were several confirmations of the event.

Garza turned his attention to other matters and the morning slipped by. As he was preparing for a lunch with the Minister of Defense, an alert flashed over his vision. It was just what he had been hoping for: a report from his contact in the Bollam's system, an admiral named Nespha.

As Garza began pouring over the data Nespha had sent in, the enormity of what had occurred in the Bollam's System struck him like a hammer blow.

A lost colony ship—*the* lost colony ship, the greatest ever built—had arrived in Bollam's World, dumped there by the Kapteyn's Streamer.

He read through the report four more times, soaking in every detail; the ship's use of impenetrable shields, the devastating attack on Hegemony Dreadnaughts—a victory so swift, he wondered how much Nespha was embellishing it. The capstone of the report was a jump to FTL; but not before the destruction of a planet, and the creation of a dark-matter-fueled black hole.

A colony ship, a *twenty-six kilometer long* colony ship, from the early fifth millennia, jumped to FTL.

There was only one possibility: The Hand had found this ship, and had taken it to the Transcend.

General Garza rose from his desk. Lunch with the secretary would be especially eventful today.

THE TRANSCEND

A LATE-NIGHT MEETING

STELLAR DATE: 05.19.8928 (Adjusted Years)
LOCATION: Transcend Interstellar Capitol
REGION: Airtha, Huygens System, Transcend Space

Mark raced through the halls of the Capitol, determined to catch Andrea before the meeting commenced.

It was late at night and the halls were nearly empty. The few people Mark did see paid him little heed; most intent on completing whatever tasks had them awake so late, and getting to bed while there was still a night to sleep through.

Mark knew that sleep would not come his way this night, and by morning—if he had his way—he would be leaving Airtha, headed to wherever *she* was.

He rounded a corner, nearly slipping on the smooth quartz floors, and spotted Andrea.

The tall, dark-haired woman moved and looked so much like her sister, that sometimes he thought she *was* Sera. However, the similarities were only skin-deep. Where Sera was earnest and determined, Andrea was cold and calculating. He greatly admired—and lusted after—Andrea, but it was Sera that he wished to possess.

"Hey! Hold up!" he called out, and Andrea turned, a scowl creasing her smooth features.

"I told you over the Link," she said with no small amount of annoyance in her voice. "You'll find out with everyone else."

Mark caught up to her and placed a hand on her shoulder. "Seriously? Me? I've known her all my life; I have a right to know."

Andrea gave his hand a venomous look that made him want her all the more, though it did have the desired effect of getting him to remove it from her soft skin.

"You don't have a right beyond anyone else. You know all you're going to until the director briefs us. Core's devils, Mark, you'll know in less than ten minutes."

Andrea turned from him and resumed her brisk walk down the corridor, and Mark rushed to keep up.

<Yeah, but I want to be prepared. I need to be on the team that goes after her.>

<Shut up, Mark. I'm not telling you anything,> Andrea punctuated her response with a sharp severing of their Link.

He sighed. "Fine."

"Fucking right, it's fine."

They rounded a corner and then turned down a narrow hall, which they followed through several security checks before reaching the entrance to their division's operations center.

Mark barely spared the main room a glance, every station still filled with personnel despite the hour, as he followed Andrea down a hall to briefing room 4C. The door slid open, and he saw that their director, Justin, was already present, seated at the head of the table. His expression was one of extreme agitation.

"Director," Mark said a moment before Andrea greeted the man by name.

"Good evening, Justin," she smiled.

"Yeah, whatever. Sit down. The other heads will be here momentarily," Director Justin grunted.

"The other heads?" Mark asked. "I thought this was a team briefing."

Justin met his eyes, the director's narrowing to slits. "Well, you thought wrong, Mark. Now sit down and shut up. This is giving me enough of a headache without having to listen to you."

Mark knew he had pushed as far as possible. Andrea hadn't been his first target that night; he had peppered the director with a host of questions when he first heard that Sera had called in.

Over the next few minutes, the other heads who were currently on Airtha filed in; for those who were away from the Capitol, AI proxies appeared to represent them.

"What's this all about?" Tressa, a section chief responsible for operations in one of the rim-ward sectors, asked. "So Seraphina called in. What about that gets us all out of bed so late?"

"Other than it being the first time she's made contact since her exile?" Andrea asked.

"Self-imposed exile," Tressa countered.

"You're right, Tressa. Sera alone would not have ruined my day so much—though she's certainly capable of such a feat if she tried," Justin sighed. "She found something, and is bringing it our way. A colony ship lost in the Kapteyn's Streamer from the fifth millennia."

Mark sat up straight and glanced around the table. Everyone had instantly become alert and attentive. They all knew how lost tech could mess up The Plan—a strategy they knew Seraphina had never fully bought into.

"What ship?" Irena asked. "There were a lot of ships lost there over the years."

Justin gave a dry laugh. "You'll know this one. It's the *Intrepid*."

It took Mark a moment to recall the ship from his days in the academy. All recruits were required to learn about lost colony ships—especially ones thought to have entered gravitational lenses. The knowledge surfaced in his mind, and he realized what was so special about this ship.

"The picotech ship," he said softly. "I thought they weren't expected to exit the streamer for another couple hundred years?"

"Correct," Justin said with a nod. "Our best guess put their exit around the year 9500. We had been building up our presence in Bollam's in preparation, but the Orion Guard knows what we know; quite the covert war has been going on there for some time."

"Which we all already know," Chief Tressa said.

"Yeah, I wasn't saying it to brief you, Tressa, it was to lead into this," Justin said as he scowled at the woman. "We have this data from multiple sources now, so what I'm about to tell you is confirmed intel…"

Mark was at a rare loss for words as he listened to the director outline the battle in the Bollam's system, and the subsequent creation of a dark matter black hole. It made their worst-case scenario for an old colony ship appearing seem like a walk in the park.

"There was no mention of the *Intrepid* having stasis shields in the accounts from Kapteyn's," Andrea said with a frown. "Are you telling us that somehow, while they were trapped in the streamer, they developed that tech?"

"You're not thinking in the right temporal frames," secretary Garrig said. "They were only in there for a few hours; maybe a couple of days at most. Whatever that shielding is, they devised it *after* coming out. I bet it was some breakthrough they made after Sera gave them grav-tech."

"How is that possible?" Mark asked. "We've never created shields like that, and, unlike the Inner Stars, we kept our tech over the last five thousand years."

"Mark, you seem to need a refresher on the early interstellar period," Justin growled. "By the time the *Intrepid* was built, it had been over four hundred years since a Worldship left Sol; that ship being the *Destiny Ascendant*. After that, we had no further interactions with the Inner Stars until after the Fall."

Mark took the criticism in stride. He didn't believe in wasting his time on ancient history. Recalling details is what AI were for, and he lived for the here and now—and the future. It was his future that concerned him most right now.

"They have a half millennia on our best source tech, not to mention whatever advantages pico gives them," Andrea said, her caustic look making Mark smile. There was just something about the woman that drove him nuts.

"They can't be that far ahead," Mark replied. "They don't have stuff like the CriEn that Sera lost; that thing being in the wild didn't cause any big ripples."

"She's lucky it didn't," Tressa said. "If it had, she wouldn't have gotten to keep flitting about out there. We'd've hauled her ass in, daddy's little girl or no."

"You would have done what you were told," a voice said from the doorway.

All eyes turned to the speaker, and Mark felt a slow smile slip across his face. Daddy's little girl, indeed. His eyes slid to the side, watching Tressa turn a dark shade of red as she stammered an apology to President Tomlinson.

"You may cease with your blathering," the president said, and waved his hand in Tressa's direction before taking a seat and looking to Justin. "So, where are we?"

"Sir," Director Justin said with a nod. "I was just about to let everyone know that Sera *did* retrieve the CriEn module and will be bringing it back with her—she bested our expectations for how long we thought it would take her, too."

Mark watched the president absorb the director's words, his brow heavy, and brooding.

"I'm glad your little experiment worked—and that she came through." The President's expression told everyone what sort of trouble Justin would be in if Sera had come to any serious harm. "Did she share it with the colonists?"

If the president's implications fazed Justin, he showed no sign of it. "We have no way of knowing. She didn't give any indication one way or the other. Our direct communication from her is brief; it confirms that the ship is the *Intrepid,* and that she is providing them with the grav-tech to make an FTL jump to Ascella."

"So, standard procedure then," the president said with a nod.

"Yes, sir."

President Tomlinson steepled his fingers and peered over them at secretary Pierce.

"Do we have a system in mind for them?"

Pierce nodded. "We've done a lot of work on the rim-ward side of M25. There's a system on the edge of the cluster that should be perfect. It has four stage-four terraformed worlds, and a dozen other planets. It would be a perfect place for them. Plus, it's only sixteen hundred light-years from Ascella, so the trip won't be too long."

"Has it already been ceded to anyone?" Tomlinson asked.

Pierce chuckled. "It's a choice system, sir. I can think of twenty groups that have their eyes on it, but no official offer has been made. To be honest, giving it to an outside group such as the *Intrepid*, would be ideal. Then I don't have to play anyone off anyone else."

"Make it happen. I would expect that the colony ship will only take four years to get there from Ascella, so we'll need to make sure the welcome mat is rolled out."

"What are we going to take in trade for a system like that?" Andrea asked. "Will we make them surrender their picotech?"

Mark watched as the president turned his attention to his daughter. "We will absolutely *not* ask for their picotech in exchange for the system. We'll take nothing beyond what they left Sol with—which is an amazing windfall in its own right."

"Sir, why the stars not?" Mark asked. "Their tech could give us an unbelievable advantage over The Orion Guard."

"We all know that the Guard has sympathizers—and likely worse—within our ranks. We need to be completely above board on this. It needs to be perfectly clear that we will not take the *Intrepid's* tech. What's more, there will be a complete embargo on directly trading any of the *Intrepid's* tech. It must all come through the DOE."

Tomlinson looked around the table as he spoke, ensuring that everyone understood what he meant. Every bit of tech from the *Intrepid* would come through the Department of Equalization, and be licensed by the federal government. There must not even be a hint of black-market trading with this colony world.

"The Guard won't believe for a second that we didn't take the pico in trade for a system," Tressa shook her head. "They'll mount an offense, and we'll have to fend them off—without the tech that they'll be after."

Tomlinson smiled.

"Now you're getting it."

"She's getting what?" Andrea asked. "Tressa's right, we need that tech and we should demand it."

"Don't be a fool," Justin said caustically— unafraid to call out the President's daughter in front of her father. "That colony ship took out four fleets in Bollam's, and bested the AST's fifth fleet afterward. And don't forget that they decimated a serious assault from the Sirians back at Kapteyn's Star. How many ships do you think we'll have to sacrifice to force them into submission?"

"We don't have to threaten them with force," Mark said, attempting to back Andrea up. "We have what they need, a colony world."

"They already built one of those at Kapteyn's Star," Secretary Pierce said. "They were prepared to fly another hundred years when they hit the Streamer and jumped forward in time. Now, with FTL, they'd just fly through the entire Transcend and find a new world, if we forced them."

Tomlinson nodded. "When they're settled and calling that world home, when The Orion Guard has mounted an offensive against us for their tech; then we'll come to them and beg for their assistance, and they'll give it to us willingly. We'll crush the Guard, and finally complete our project."

"So long as Seraphina doesn't mess things up," Andrea growled. "She's like a plasma bomb in situations like this."

The president cast an appraising eye at his daughter. "Then you'll bring her back to Airtha. I will explain the situation to her."

"*I'll* bring her back?" Andrea said, distaste dripping from her voice. "I really don't fancy taking half a year out of my life to go meet with my errant sister. Send Mark, they have history together."

Mark held a smile back. Being the one sent to meet with Seraphina was the only thing that mattered to him right now. If she had the CriEn module, he would have to destroy it...or her...or both. Given the risks, both would probably be best.

He realized that the president was giving him an appraising look and hoped none of his thoughts had shown on his face.

"I'm no fool, Mark," Tomlinson said. "I read the reports about what happened when your team lost the CriEn—when you lost Seraphina. I don't think that you're the best option. Andrea, it's you. Bring Serge as well. At least he actually likes Seraphina; it'll help smooth things over."

* * * * *

"For fuck's sake," Andrea muttered as she walked the halls of the Capitol. "Of all the fucking stupid things to get pulled into, I have to go fetch my dumbass sister from half way across the Arm."

<Could be worse,> her AI, Gerard, broke into her tirade.

<Oh yeah? How's that? Do I have to cut my own arms off too? I think that's about what it would take to have it be worse.>

<Well,> Gerard used his most placating tone, which Andrea hated, but tolerated since Gerard was brilliant and almost always a boon to her plans. <She could have lost the ship to the Hegemony in that battle. It was some gutsy stuff she pulled off, what with driving her ship right through a shield bubble.>

<That whole battle was one risky move stacked on another. That Tanis Richards is a menace; bringing her to the Transcend is a horrible idea,> Andrea surprised herself with the venom in her mental tone. Well, the woman did kill her pet asset in the Bollam's system. Admiral Senya had been a woman after Andrea's own heart. She had spent some time shaping her future to ensure a strong military in the system—a necessary element to back New Eden against the Hegemony.

<Then you'll be happy to know that we have orders regarding her,> Gerard said conspiratorially. <She's

not to make it to their colony system. Your father doesn't want her in the Transcend any more than you do. Our patterners can't discern her path well enough. She's too powerful, and too unpredictable.>

Andrea laughed aloud, feeling a sense of joy for the first time since getting the intelligence about the battle in Bollam's World.

<Well then; now that this is a challenge, instead of a babysitting mission, it's becoming a bit more interesting.>

PREPARATION

STELLAR DATE: 05.20.8928 (Adjusted Years)
LOCATION: High Airtha Port
REGION: Airtha, Huygens System, Transcend Space

"So what's this about?" a voice asked from behind Andrea as she reviewed the ship's pre-flight status. She turned to see her second-youngest brother, Serge, standing at the entrance of the small bridge.

"Serge," she said by way of greeting. "No one briefed you?"

The stocky man shook his head. "Nope, Director Justin told me to hit you up when I got on board. What's the deal?"

"We're getting Sera," Andrea replied simply. "She picked up a colony ship out of Kapteyn's Streamer—details are on the bridge net in the mission dossier."

Serge took a seat at a console and pulled up the mission details. Andrea let him read in peace; she had enough to do, if they were to leave in the next hour. Satisfied that the pre-flight checks had all met her exacting standards, she moved on to assessing the supplies and weapons loadout. Chances were that any combat would be minimal—likely just infiltration and a quick strike, if it came to that.

"Well, then, it's like a reunion," another voice said from the bridge's entrance. "Just like old times."

Andrea's head whipped around to see Mark standing on her bridge, that insufferable smile on his face. The man thought he was causality's gift to the cosmos, and flaunted his obnoxious personality wherever he went. Her sister's one-time infatuation with him had lowered Sera in Andrea's estimation, more than anything else the impetuous girl had ever done.

Still, almost by some miracle, he managed to get results, and so The Hand kept him around. It would seem that one of his "results" was his presence on the bridge.

"What are you doing here?" Andrea snapped.

"You didn't think I'd take that dismissal lying down, did you?" Mark asked. "I convinced Justin that even though Sera and I didn't separate on the best of terms, I know her well and can be of use. I've spent more time with her in the field than either of you. So, Justin convinced the president, and here I am."

Andrea left out a long-suffering sigh. "Fine. Make yourself useful. We need another thousand liters of saline, and food for another person. Get a service mech to top us off, and take care of your supplies."

Mark scowled at the menial task but left to perform it without a word.

<Check to make sure he's approved to be here,> Andrea ordered.

<I already did,> Gerard replied. <He's on the up and up.>

<Well, shit.>

"Going to be fun, listening to him talk about how awesome he is for this whole mission," Serge said without looking up from the reports he was poring over.

"Looks like he's not supposed to be in the initial meet, though," Andrea said. "At least father had the sense to see how bad that would be."

"This looks pretty nuts," Serge said from his console. "Do you think this ship really has pico and stasis shields? It's like finding two holy grails—it's a bit hard to believe."

Andrea nodded. "Alternative postulations are welcome—though, so far, no one has any. The ship survived a direct hit from a black hole's relativistic jet. Nothing short of a star should survive that kind of punishment."

"So a world for their tech then, eh?" Serge asked as he stood and walked to Andrea's side, examining their route on the holoprojection.

"Yup, standard deal for an old colony ship—though at least this one will actually be worth it," Andrea replied.

"It's not supposed to work in our favor, Andrea," Serge said with a frown. "Making worlds for these colonists is what the FGT was founded to do. Just because some of them got lost along the way, doesn't mean we can't help them."

"Yeah, I know you see it that way," Andrea said. "But you're being naïve. Those colonists *already* had worlds made for them. Just because they broke down or got lost on the way, doesn't mean that we have to give up our choice worlds now."

"The *Intrepid* didn't get lost, at least not in space," Serge replied. "It's poetic justice really, that they showed up at Bollam's and gave them what for."

Andrea nodded in agreement. Serge may be a romantic, but he was right about that. The original colonists at Bollam's world, also dumped there by the Kapteyn's Streamer, had originally set out from

Sirius, headed to New Eden; intent on stealing it from the *Intrepid* before the colony ship arrived.

Given the fleet and weaponry that the *Intrepid's* colonists had created for themselves while at Kapteyn's Star, she imagined that the colony thieves from Sirius would have been in for quite the surprise—if either of them had ever made it to New Eden.

"I wonder if Sera will be the same?" Serge asked wistfully. "It must have been rough—what happened to her."

Andrea snorted. "What? Royally fucking up, getting her support team killed, losing invaluable tech, and then running away and taking up work as a freighter captain?"

"That's a skewed view. You know that she wasn't fully responsible for that," Serge replied.

"Yeah, Mark may be an asshat, but at least he came back and took his licks. She ran away."

Serge gave Andrea a hard look. "She's still our sister, our code."

Andrea snorted. "She's *your* sister. I'm a thousand years older than you two—and we don't share the same mother. I'd like to think that I share as little genetic code as possible with Seraphina."

Neither spoke for a minute before Serge stood and approached the holo tank.

"Looks like it'll take us just over seven months to get there," he said, apparently also interested in changing the topic.

"Yeah, we'll punch a hole to the edge of the Corona Australis cloud, and then fly through the dark layer to get to Ascella. We'll do a few course corrections as well—doesn't' hurt to be safe. That ship probably has the AST searching everywhere for it."

Serge nodded. "And I assume that the Watchpoint has been alerted?"

"Yes, a full assault force will be pulled from stasis—just in case."

"Good," Mark said from the doorway. "If I know Sera, we may just need it."

SINGULARITY

UNREST
STELLAR DATE: 02.29.8928 (Adjusted Years)
LOCATION: ISS *Intrepid*
REGION: Interstellar Dark Layer below the Galactic Disk

<Angela?> Tanis asked her AI, deep in the darkness one sleepless night.

<What is it?> her AI responded, always alert and ready to converse.

<Is what's happening to us putting ou — my daughter at risk?>

Angela paused before she responded. Tanis could tell because she could count the milliseconds, and knew her AI had taken almost fifteen more than her norm.

<I don't think so,> Angela replied. Her DNA looks perfectly normal; her brain development is perfectly natural.

<I know that,> Tanis said. *<I can **see** her DNA. But that's just the thing. Who can see their child's DNA in their minds?>*

<Well, it's not that hard, really,> Angela said.

<Ang, stop equivocating. You know what I mean. I'm not using the Link to see it; I'm not directly inserting the

visuals of a simulation into my mind. I can see it. I can see my cells, I can see every part of my body.>

<You've been able to do that for some time—decades—why is it bothering you now?>

Tanis reached down and stroked her distended stomach, feeling the life growing inside shift about. Beside her, Joe stirred and she stilled herself. There was no need to disrupt his sleep as well.

<Call it instinct, whatever, I just know that there's this small life inside me now…and it's my…everything to keep it safe. No one will ever know her like I will. It's like she'll always be a part of me—but what if we pass on…whatever it is that makes us what we are, to her?>

<Then she'll be lucky, if you'll pardon the pun,> Angela said with a smile.

<Har har, you're a bucket of laughs.>

<I learned from the best,> Angela replied. <But seriously; we've surmounted the most unbelievable odds so far, and always come out on top. We're at the end of that struggle now. We can look forward to hundreds of years of rest and relaxation—we'll get to grow old together.>

<AIs don't grow old,> Tanis replied with a smile.

<Maybe I'll give it a shot with you,> Angela responded.

<Ang...what is happening to us?> Tanis asked, a small amount of worry in her mental tone.

<I don't know,> Angela replied. *<No one knows, not even Bob. But it's beautiful, and I love you, so I know it's going to be all right.>*

<I love you too, Angela,> Tanis said with a sigh. She hadn't really expected an answer. She and Angela co-thought a lot about what was happening to them, and neither really knew. *<OK...I think I'm going to try sleeping again. Keep it quiet out there in the Expanse. I can hear it, you know.>*

<I know, I'll do my best to buffer the noise,> the AI said softly.

<Thanks, Ang.>

The Story Continues in New Canaan
Now available on Amazon

THANK YOU

If you've enjoyed reading Set the Galaxy on Fire, a review on Amazon.com and/or goodreads.com would be greatly appreciated.

To get the latest news and access to free novellas and short stories, sign up on the Aeon 14 mailing list: www.aeon14.com/signup.

M. D. Cooper

BOOKS BY M. D. COOPER

Aeon 14

The Intrepid Saga

- Book 1: Outsystem
- Book 2: A Path in the Darkness
- Book 3: Building Victoria
- The Intrepid Saga Omnibus – *Also contains Destiny Lost, book 1 of the Orion War series*
- Destiny Rising – *Special Author's Extended Edition comprised of both Outsystem and A Path in the Darkness with over 100 pages of new content.*

The Orion War

- Book 1: Destiny Lost
- Tales of the Orion War: Set the Galaxy on Fire
- Book 2: New Canaan
- Book 3: Orion Rising
- Tales of the Orion War: Ignite the Stars Within (Fall 2017)
- Tales of the Orion War: Burn the Galaxy to Ash (Fall 2017)
- Book 4: Starfire (coming in 2018)
- Book 5: Return to Sol (coming in 2018)

  Visit www.aeon14.com/orionwar to learn what's next in the Orion War.

Perilous Alliance (Expanded Orion War - with Chris J. Pike)

- Book 1: Close Proximity
- Book 2: Strike Vector (August 2017)
- Book 3: Collision Course (October 2017)

Rika's Marauders (Age of the Orion War)

- Prequel: Rika Mechanized
- Book 1: Rika Outcast (August 2017)

Perseus Gate (Age of the Orion War)
- Episode 1: The Gate at the Grey Wolf Star
- Episode 2: The World at the Edge of Space (July 2017)
- Episode 3: The Dance on the Moons of Serenity (August 2017)

The Warlord (Before the Age of the Orion War)
- Book 1: A Woman Without a Country (Sept 2017)

The Sentience Wars: Origins (With James S. Aaron)
- Book 1: Lyssa's Dream (July 2017)
- Book 2: Lyssa's Run (October 2017)

The Sol Dissolution
- The 242 - Venusian Uprising (In The Expanding Universe 2 anthology)
- The 242 - Assault on Tarja (In The Expanding Universe 2 anthology – coming Dec 2017)

The Delta Team Chronicles (Expanded Orion War)
- A "Simple" Kidnapping (Pew! Pew! Volume 1)
- The Disney World (Pew! Pew! Volume 2 – Sept 2017)

Touching the Stars

Book 1: The Girl Who Touched the Stars

APPENDICES

Be sure to check http://www.aeon14.com for the latest information on the Aeon 14 universe.

ABOUT THE AUTHOR

Michael Cooper likes to think of himself as a jack-of-all-trades (and hopes to become master of a few). When not writing, he can be found writing software, working in his shop at his latest carpentry project, or likely reading a book.

He shares his home with a precocious young girl, his wonderful wife (who also writes), two cats, a never-ending list of things he would like to build, and ideas...

Find out what's coming next at www.aeon14.com

91157246R00117

Made in the USA
Columbia, SC
13 March 2018